Follow

your

Heart

Follow your Heart

TASHA NATHAN

JAMES LORIMER & COMPANY LTD., PUBLISHERS
TORONTO

James Lorimer & Company Ltd., Publishers acknowledges the support of
the Ontario Arts Council (OAC), an agency of the Government of Ontario,
which in 2015-16 funded 1,676 individual artists and 1,125 organizations in
209 communities across Ontario for a total of $50.5 million. We acknowledge
the support of the Canada Council for the Arts, which last year invested $153
million to bring the arts to Canadians throughout the country. This project
has been made possible in part by the Government of Canada and with the
support of the Ontario Media Development Corporation.

Cover design: Tyler Cleroux
Cover image: Shutterstock

Library and Archives Canada Cataloguing in Publication

Nathan, Tasha, author
    Follow your heart / Tasha Nathan.

Issued in print and electronic formats.
ISBN 978-1-4594-1214-9 (paperback).--ISBN 978-1-4594-1216-3 (epub)

    I. Title.

PS8627.A793F65 2017   jC813'.6   C2016-906055-1
                                               C2016-906056-X

Published by: Distributed by:
James Lorimer & Company Ltd.,   Formac Lorimer Books
Publishers   5502 Atlantic Street
117 Peter Street, Suite 304   Halifax, NS, Canada
Toronto, ON, Canada   B3H 1G4
M5V 0M3
www.lorimer.ca

Printed and bound in Canada.
Manufactured by Friesens Corporation in Altona, Manitoba, Canada in
January 2017.
Job #229626

For my mother and father,
thank you for your
never-ending faith and support.

01 Inner Storm

WHEN DID IT START? When did I start pouring out all my feelings into my blog, *Confessions of a Sri Lankan Girl*? As a Tamil teen, I needed an outlet for my feelings about the obedience my culture and my family demanded. Doing what my parents wanted seemed easier when I was younger. I rarely went out with friends. Instead, book girl that I am, I focused on keeping an A+ average at school. Going with my parents to whatever events they wanted took up the rest of my time. But as the years passed, I started feeling a tightness in my chest every time I heard my parents say to me, "Tamil girls don't do that." They said it as if that was enough for me to drop the idea of anything I wanted for myself. But it wasn't enough anymore. More and more, I watched my few friends go on to live a life of their choosing. I watched them move on without me. I felt stuck and I was starting to hate it.

I heard my mom talking on the phone with one of her many friends. They were gossiping about the daughter of another friend, a girl about my age who had been seen with a guy by someone else in the Tamil community. My mom was clearly shocked, but she loved the gossip. The way they talked, it was as if the girl and her boyfriend had been caught having sex in public. And it was clearly all the girl's fault, as far as Mom and her friend thought. I rolled my eyes and talked to my mom as soon as she was off the phone.

I couldn't let her get away with demonizing the poor girl. And the double standard made it even worse. It was clear that my mom and her friend blamed the girl, not her boyfriend, for letting things go so far. I pointed out to my mom that there were plenty of Tamil boys in my school who had one or more girlfriends, and they had no problem getting physical with them in public, so they must go further in private.

She waved away my words with her hands. "Nisha, they are boys, they will always be boys," she explained. "It is the girls who have to be good, have to stay pure. It's up to Prema to maintain her purity and reputation."

I looked at her as if she was an alien speaking an unknown language. Who was this person, with her unfair opinion? Where was my mom, who always told me I would make her proud by doing well in school and making something of myself? "What do you mean?" I asked. Surely there was some weird explanation for what my mom was telling me. Did what she was saying go for me too?

"A girl has to misbehave only once for the guy to know she's impure. But it's different for boys. You have to expect that they will try to get as much as they can, in any situation. Boys can get themselves dirty many times and still have a clean reputation. That's why girls have to be so careful."

I stared at my mom. I think my mouth was open in surprise. I tried to understand what she was saying, what my mom was telling me about her view of the world. But I simply couldn't. As the shock of her words wore off, I felt the first hint of anger emerge. I bit my lips, trying to hold in the words I wanted to yell at her. That's how I found myself in front of my laptop. My fingers were flying over the keyboard of my laptop. Words formed on the screen in front of me. The letters twisted across the page like the confusion I felt inside. My thoughts fuelled my anger as I pounded on the keys. If I didn't, I was sure that a scream would erupt from my lips.

The click of the keyboard was the only sound in the room. I continued to type about the double standards and lack of fairness between men and women that made me almost hate the culture I was born into. As I typed, I felt my anger seep into my writing, releasing me from the knot of confusion and resentment I had tied myself into. I had spent years being silent and accepting what I had seen and been taught. But I found I could express and work through my emotions by writing them down.

When I was done, when all the feelings I had were on the screen instead of in my heart, I paused. I took a deep breath and quickly read over what I had written. I had to make sure that the words were perfect. I had to make sure that they were a true reflection of what I thought and felt. I had to make sure that they would speak to the reader. I pressed publish on the account that was linked to my blog, *Confessions of a Sri Lankan Girl*.

After a few minutes of browsing through my other posts I logged off and stared at the black screen. It was the last weekend of summer and this would be my last year of high school. I opened up my desk drawer and took out a folded piece of paper. It was my class schedule for the week.

The door to my room opened. I turned to see my mother.

"*Amma*, why don't you ever knock? Why do you just barge in?" I asked. Her lack of respect for my privacy — and for me — made me angry again.

"Your *Appa* and I pay for this house, for this door. I don't need to knock. When you start helping to pay the mortgage and bills, then we can have this conversation again."

I glared at her but didn't say anything. I told myself not to let the anger take control again. I held my tongue.

"What is it?" my voice was cold and curt.

"Nisha, I need to know what's the problem?" She didn't speak gently, as you would expect a parent to out of concern for a loved daughter. Instead, my mother talked down to me, as if I were not important. Her years of experience as a nursing teacher in Sri Lanka and Oman made her ways of teaching and parenting different from what was normal in the West. Her tone was arrogant and patronizing. It really didn't improve my already irritated mood.

"Nothing," I replied.

"Then why did you give me that attitude downstairs?" she demanded.

"What attitude?"

"That attitude when I was talking about Prema."

"Nothing." I turned back to my laptop. As I did I felt a smack at the back of my head.

"Don't turn your back to me. When I ask you a question, you must answer it." I turned to see my mom standing with arms crossed, glaring at me.

"Fine. You want to know what's wrong? I really didn't like the double standard you and your friend showed when talking about Prema. I can't believe you, as an 'educated' person," I held my fingers up in air quotes around the word, "would think it's completely okay to say something like that!"

"It is the girl who protects the honour of the home. If she goes around with guys, not only is she shaming her family, she is destroying her life," my mother bit out.

I threw my hands up in the air. "For god's sakes,

why the hell did you come here? Why bring me to Canada if you are going to mentally be tied to where we come from? You do realize that schools here are not gender separated? Girls and boys do study together and also, oh my god," I said with a fake shocked expression, "work together as you do."

"Nisha, looking at boys and girls this way is part of our culture. And as long as you are part of our culture and this household, you will do what we tell you."

I shook my head in anger. My jaw clenched as I tried to hold back a scream. But instead of talking back, I just stared at her for a moment. I tried to calm myself before I spoke.

02 Fluttering Hearts

"IS THERE ANYTHING ELSE YOU NEEDED?" I asked my mother.

"You have school tomorrow. What are the classes?"

"For tomorrow I have Creative Writing, Geometry, and English."

"Only three? I thought the school day had four classes."

"I have a spare in between."

"What other courses are you taking?"

"Why are you asking me? You and *Appa* are the ones that picked my courses for me. You should know."

She looked at me with a disapproving stare. She didn't have to say a word to warn me to watch what I said to her.

Part of me wanted to poke at her to see how far I could go. But I had endured years of being hit — with a hand, a book, whatever was close at hand — for disobeying even the slightest thing. I decided I'd rather not go to school the next day with any red marks on my body. With a resigned sigh, I told her, "Biology, Law, Accounting, and then another spare."

"I still don't know why you need to take Creative Writing on top of English," she grumbled. "Other more serious courses would have been far better. Chemistry would have been better." She pursed her lips as she thought of the time I was "wasting" on writing.

"It's an easy A, *Amma*. And improving my writing skills will always be useful with my other studies."

She shrugged and nodded. But I could tell she didn't really accept my reasons. "Okay go to bed early.

Appa will drop you." And with that she left the room, closing my bedroom door behind her.

I glared at the door a few more seconds before I gave up being angry. With a sigh I got ready for bed. I lay in the dark room, my eyes slowly adjusting to the darkness. I looked up at the ceiling and wondered why I couldn't just accept what my parents were trying to tell me. It would make life easier, and maybe I'd be happier. But the more I tried to, the more I felt like a trapped animal scrambling for freedom.

I thought about Prema. I felt sorry for her. If she was anything like me, she didn't need or deserve the judgement. Her mysterious guy could have just been a friend or classmate, or even a stranger asking for directions. But I knew South Asians, they loved to twist the truth for entertainment. It offered a chance for good gossip at the expense of another person's reputation.

As I drifted off to sleep, my last thought was a passionate but hopeless wish that I had been born into a different life.

I sat by my locker, drumming a pencil against the notebook I had on my lap. I was looking for inspiration but nothing came. My father had dropped me at school a half an hour too early. Unsure how else to occupy my time, I plopped myself on the floor and tried to doodle. I was bored after making a few strokes, and was left watching students walk by. There was a feeling of excitement as students reunited with their friends after the summer. The chatter of gossip, and stories of summer adventures, slowly grew as the clock counted down to the first bell of the school year. I heard shrieks of excitement and laughter. I could easily tell who were the newbies just entering the big, bad world of high school. The seniors were striding the halls with confidence. It was as if entering the final year was proof of their ability to conquer the world. I felt a pang of envy, wishing that I shared in that confidence. Instead, I felt more like a puppet caught up in strings other people were holding.

My eyes caught sight of a boy and girl hugging each other near the end of the hall. They were brown, or South Asian, and I knew the girl was Tamil. By the looks of it, they hadn't seen each other the whole summer. The girl was in a few of my classes last year. I recalled hearing that her parents almost never allowed her to leave the house unless they, or one of her siblings, were with her. But her parents couldn't keep her from school, and here she was — with a boy. They looked like there was no one in the world apart from each other. I felt a small smile of approval cross my face. What would it be like to feel so close to another person that anyone could tell by looking at you? I found myself wishing I knew what it was like to feel the arms of a boy wrap around me.

Not just any boy, either. My thoughts drifted to Todd Miller. I felt warmth fill my heart as an image of my long-time crush filled my head. Where other girls gossiped and gasped at pictures of celebrities, my daydreams were filled with Todd. The first time I saw him, it was in grade nine Art. He was tall with an athletic build, but what struck me most were his warm brown eyes. He was a star on the soccer team, as well as one of the smartest kids in school — beauty and brains. Despite all that, he seemed humble. He had a charm that could make any girl blush, but seemed not to be aware of his effect on other people. That's what got me curious about him at first. Although Todd had been in a few of the same classes as I was, we never exchanged more than a few words. That was mostly due to my shyness, but he was warm and respectful to me anyway. My feelings for him had deepened as I saw his kindness during the tsunami that had hit Southeast Asia. Todd had spearheaded a fundraising effort to collect money to give to charities helping the affected countries. His caring attitude spread as he used his contacts in sports and social activities to make others aware of how they could help. Todd was different from any boy I had ever seen, white or brown, and he made my heart melt.

Suddenly eager to see him, my eyes searched the bustling hallway as I began gathering my books.

I made my way to Creative Writing, hoping to catch a glimpse of him. As my classroom got closer, I stifled my disappointment at not being able to start my school day with the sight of Todd.

It was as if the universe decided to answer my wish, and more. I entered the classroom and stopped dead in my tracks at the sight of Todd sitting in the front corner desk. I quickly took a step back to check the number on the door and make sure I had the right classroom. When I saw that I did, I slowly walked all the way in. There was an empty seat right next to Todd. I pushed any doubts out of my mind and boldly decided to take it. As I tried to get comfortable in my seat, I couldn't help but glance Todd's way. To my surprise, I saw that he was looking at me, smiling as our eyes met. My heart was thudding, but I somehow managed to give him a half-smile before quickly looking away. I pretended to focus on the book in front of me.

Students were still pouring in and a few minutes later the bell rang. I could hear the sound of other kids chattering as they prepared for class. The teacher hadn't arrived yet. I took a quick look around and realized the class wasn't as full as I had thought it would be. There were only around fifteen students, and I was glad for the small class size. If we were going to be doing presentations, my anxiety level would be better if the classroom wasn't filled. I reached into my bag and took out my notebook. Then, with another quick glance at Todd, I turned my attention to the front of the room, waiting for class to start.

03 Uncharted Ground

THE TEACHER CAME IN just as the bell rang. She was a petite, Asian woman with shoulder length, straight black hair and thick, black-framed glasses. She had a bright smile on her face that put me at ease right away. "Hello class! My name is Mrs. Chou and I will be your teacher for Creative Writing." She walked up to the blackboard and scribbled her name with the white chalk. Then she turned around and clasped her hands, smiling as she looked around at us. "Let's get started right away with writing. As an introduction I want all of you to write a bit about yourself. I want your writing to get the reader really interested in you as an individual. Facts are fine, but they should be chosen so that they say something about you." She paused. "Then pick a partner to share what you wrote with. Make sure it's someone who you've never spent time with and is not one of your friends. We need to see how well you have succeeded in your writing."

Before I could look around and see who I could ask to be my partner, I felt a tap on my arm. Todd was leaning over to me. "You want to be partners?" he asked.

My tongue seemed frozen from nervousness. So I quickly nodded in response and gave him a smile. He smiled back and then started searching his binder for a piece of paper.

I sat there, not needing to move since my partner was sitting right beside me. I took a piece of paper out of my binder and started writing. I had to make this good, something that would make me seem interesting to the reader. Something that would make me interesting to Todd.

I was born in the midst of a civil war in Sri Lanka. My parents left me with my aunt as they tried to settle in a different country. Their biggest aim was to find a place to provide me with some stability in an unstable world. I remember seeing the military army passing through our fields once. My aunt led me to safety, hiding in the house. It's funny how nothing else from my childhood was etched into my mind as much as that memory.

Sri Lanka was surrounded by natural beauty, with mountains, trees, and beautiful beaches. But the stench of poverty and war marred the country, which had once been like a paradise. Every day you would go about your day in fear of a potential attack. Along with that fear, feelings were clouded by a never-ending, ever-growing hatred between the Sinhalese and Tamils. The Sri Lankan government ordered that each home in Northern Sri Lanka must have a bunker. They were built so that families could take cover from the shelling.

The only place that seemed to be free of falling bombs was the city. However, travelling from the countryside to the city was a long and stressful journey. The ride there was dotted with military checkpoints, the government army as well as the Tamil Tigers, the militant organization that had taken over Northern Sri Lanka.

My parents were able to get me out of Sri Lanka, as the war got worse, to Oman. I remember growing up in Oman, surrounded by the luxury the oil-rich country had to provide. Everywhere you looked there was decadence, and all you could feel was heat. Although Sri Lanka was hot, it was not the dry heat that scorched the Middle Eastern desert. I remember thinking I could probably cook an egg on the pavement because you couldn't step out barefoot without burning your foot. Here, what lacked in nature was made up for with man-made beauty. There were sandy beaches that we visited every weekend and lots of delicious foods. It was very different compared to the life we lived in Sri Lanka. Poverty was not a common experience. The Omani all seemed to have an air of arrogance. They knew they were born into privilege.

As much as we loved living in Oman, there was still a lot of racism. It didn't matter that we lived there for almost five years. We could never own property or become citizens. And *getting a good education wasn't an option for someone whose skin was darker than the Omanis. Foreigners, especially those from South Asian and African countries, often lived in bad conditions. Rooms with no air conditioning, months without pay and, for those who worked as maids and other household help, often severe abuse from their employers. We were the lucky ones, as both my parents worked for the government. But the fact that we were treated with more respect didn't make the racism any better.*

I stopped there. How much was too much to give away? I turned to look at Todd, who was still writing. I debated with myself about adding more, but decided against it. Mrs. Chou said it should be interesting. How interesting would the thoughts of a Sri Lankan girl be to someone like Todd? Still lost in my memories, I was jolted out of my thoughts when Todd gently touched my arm to get my attention.

"You done?" he asked.

"Yeah," I nodded. We traded papers to read each other's work.

What Todd wrote was pretty much what I expected. He started off with his family, where he grew up, and his likes and dislikes. I smiled as I read that he liked to read and that his favourite thing to do was to browse online blogs. He listed some of his favourite blog sites and as I went down the list my breath stopped at one entry. *Confessions of a Sri Lankan Girl. He's white,* I thought, *why in the word would be interested in a blog like that?*

I sneaked a peek his way, wondering if I should even bother with my question. I saw he was reading my paper and nearing the end. I decided if I didn't ask him, it would bug me the rest of the day. "Hey," I said to get his attention. I paused long enough for him to raise his eyes to my face before I went on. "Just out of curiosity, why did you list *Confessions of a Sri Lankan Girl* as one of your favourite blogs?"

"Why shouldn't I read it?"

"It's interesting that you would take a liking to something when it didn't have any cultural significance to you."

He responded with a simple shrug. "I don't know.

I like it. It's different from the other things I read," he said. "I'm in a school where seventy-five percent of students are brown. I started reading it because I thought it would be nice to know how they thought and felt. But once I started reading some of them, it was like the bloggers became my friends."

I stared at him. His answer did not satisfy me. It even kind of irritated me. He made it sound like brown people were a species that he wanted to learn about. I don't know if it made it better or worse that the blog he liked was my blog. And how was I supposed to feel when he said that reading my blog made us friends? Especially when I'd wanted to know him for so long.

"If you want to know how brown people feel," I asked, "why don't you try talking to them? Do you really think that reading a blog is the same as knowing someone?"

He sensed the note of anger in my voice and tried to explain. "If the writing is really well done, it comes close to knowing the blogger. Isn't that why people write?" he countered.

Before I could think of a good way to reply, the teacher stopped the partner talk. "Okay class, I want you to hand in what you wrote. I'm going to read them and I'll give feedback to each of you next class. Class dismissed."

I collected my things and grabbed my paper off the table before Todd could say anything. I hurried to the teacher's desk to drop off the paper and practically ran out of class.

"Nisha, wait," I could hear Todd yell behind me. I picked up my pace. I didn't want to talk to him, after spending all that time longing for just that. How could our first conversation have gone so badly? I rounded the hallway and quickly went through the double doors and up the staircase. I stopped for a few seconds to see if Todd was going to follow me through the doors, but the doorway was just filled with other students. Breathing a sigh of relief, I slowed my pace and went to my next class.

04 Strangers to Friends

I STARED AT MY LOCKER. I was tired and just for once I wanted to do something fun. But what could I do before classes started? Fidgeting with the lock, I played with the idea of skipping my first class. But I decided it wasn't worth it. If my parents found out there would be all sorts of questions thrown at me. They would start with empty accusations that I was seeing a boy on the sly, and move on to being angry with me for not caring enough about school. With a sigh, I closed my locker. Then I almost let out a scream when I felt someone standing really close behind me.

My hand to my chest, I briefly closed my eyes to gather my wits. I opened them to stare right into Todd's eyes. He was standing in front of me with an amused expression on his face.

"Oh hell, Todd! You scared me! Why didn't you say anything?" I demanded.

"You seemed like you were thinking about something important. I didn't want to interrupt."

I glared at him, my lips thinning as I thought about how silly I must have looked.

Holding up his hands as if to ward off my displeasure, he said, "Okay, okay, fine I'm sorry." There was a note of laughter in his voice. But all I could do was glare.

"What do you want?" I asked. We hadn't spoken since I ran out of the classroom after Creative Writing. To tell the truth, I felt a bit foolish for overreacting. And now, despite my irritation, a big part of me was excited to see him. I felt the warmth of happiness wash over me at the sound of his voice.

He scratched the back of his head, and looked at me sheepishly. "I wanted to know if you and I were cool. I mean, I don't want you think that just because I read that blog I don't actually talk with people who are non-white. It's just nice to get a better understanding of cultural differences before I say or do something weird or offensive. I don't want to assume things when I talk with people who are different from me. Like you're different, Nisha."

What did that mean? The way he was smiling made me think that maybe different wasn't so bad. "That makes sense . . . and we're cool." I gave him a small smile. "I admit I overreacted. And what you said about writing actually made me think."

"So . . . friends?" he said as he held his hand out for me to shake.

Laughing, I shook his hand. "Yes . . . friends!"

I felt like I was walking on the clouds. Here was a guy that I had liked since freshman year. A guy who I didn't think knew I was alive. And now we were friends. I had a feeling it would be a good day.

"What do you have now?" he asked me as we walked down the hall together.

"Accounting," I said, rolling my eyes.

"Yuck, why did you pick that?"

"I didn't, my parents did."

He looked at me in disbelief. "Your parents picked your courses?"

I nodded, staring at my feet. I felt stupid for sharing that information. *He probably thinks that I'm an idiot for not being able to pick my own classes.* "Yeah . . . they are very strict about me getting into a good university and the right program. So they want to make sure I take the right courses now."

"Have they always done that?"

"Since grade nine," I admitted. It hadn't been a fun four years. But fighting them just seemed like too much work, so I went along with whatever they had picked for me.

"And you're okay with it?" he asked, still looking shocked by what I was telling him.

I shrugged. "It doesn't make a difference whether

34   FOLLOW YOUR HEART

I am. But they mean well . . ." I didn't know what else to say. It was one thing to feel and write about how my parents' control of my life bothered me. But telling someone I hardly knew felt like I was betraying them.

Todd let out a low whistle. "Damn . . . that wouldn't be okay with me." He paused. "Wait, so they picked the Creative Writing class for you too?"

I shook my head. "No, I had to convince them. I already had most of the science credits, so I told them it would be an easy A. It was the only way for me to get a class that I actually want for myself."

He nodded, "I'm glad you're in that class."

I was a bit surprised. "Why?"

"'Cause you have a talent for it. And you seemed to enjoy writing."

"I do . . . I dunno it's like a release for me."

"Yeah . . . I can understand that. When you come from 'a culture that does not encourage independence, one that is entrenched in community at the expense of individuality,' it can be a bit stifling. At least, I would think so."

I stared at him, perplexed. I could tell he was quoting. But what was he quoting?

"What? I told you I read a lot," he said with a chuckle.

I shook my head in wonder. But I also felt a smile form on lips as I felt myself liking this guy more and more.

"Your understanding of South Asian culture is pretty impressive," I observed.

He shrugged, "The girl that I like comes from that background. Reading about it helps me understand her . . . at least, I hope it does."

My heart sank. Of course there was someone that Todd liked. He never looked like he had a girlfriend, but maybe she just didn't go to our school. Even so, part of me had hoped that he felt the same way as me. I gave myself a mental slap as I forced myself to not react. I swallowed the lump that was forming in my throat.

Even though Todd had spoken casually, his eyes were still on me. I was suddenly aware that I needed to hide the expression on my face. Wanting to create space between us, I looked at my phone. I feigned a surprised expression. "I have to go. I completely forgot I had to meet my teacher to ask her something before my next class." I gave Todd a bright fake smile as I turned and hurried away. But my last glance back confirmed I was leaving behind a very confused Todd.

05 To Have or Not to Have

AS WE WALKED INTO THE HOME of my aunt Keera and uncle Kumar, I could hear Keera Aunty yelling in the background. The house was filled with the sounds of little children laughing and screaming as they ran around. Men's laughter could be heard coming through the basement door. The women were grouped in the living room chatting while Keera Aunty scurried around the kitchen preparing the lunch dishes.

As I entered, Keera Aunty hurried over. Her arms were stretched out wide to trap me in a hug. "Hallo, Daaling," she drawled in her South Asian accent.

"Hi, Aunty," I said shyly after she pulled away.

She ushered me to the living room. "Go have a seat, I'll bring you some tea. Or would you rather go upstairs? Reshanthy and Thurka are there." She was referring to her teenage daughters. The next moment her voice switched to a scream as she called down to the basement at her husband, "KUMAR CAN YOU GET THE CHICKEN AND BRING IT UP? I CAN'T DO EVERYTHING BY MYSELF YOU KNOW!"

I was surprised by her sudden change in tone, even though it was familiar. I wondered if it was a South Asian trait. Did all South Asian moms have a talent for switching personalities at the blink of an eye? "KUMAR!" she screamed again even louder. She was shrieking so loud, her voice sounded scratchy. I watched her shake her head and grumble under her breath, brows furrowed in anger. I almost felt sorry for my uncle. Almost.

I ran up the stairs and walked into Reshanthy's bedroom. Reshanthy, Thurka, and two other girls I didn't know were lounging on the bed and chairs. As I walked into the familiar room, they greeted me with a chorus of heys. Reshanthy smiled and waved me towards an empty space on the bed.

I sat down and got myself comfortable. "So . . . what's up . . . what are you guys talking about?" I asked, feeling a bit like an intruder.

"Nothing much. Devi was just telling us about her boyfriend," said Thurka.

"Oh, you have a boyfriend?" I knew that most of the girls dated boys, but usually no one serious enough to call a boyfriend.

Devi nodded her head. "Yeah, we've been dating for about six months." She took out her phone and showed me a picture of herself with her boyfriend. They had their arms around each other and they were laughing. He was brown skinned with thick, black hair and a trimmed goatee. He wasn't movie star attractive, but there was confidence in his smile and that made him attractive. *He must work out a lot,* I thought as I looked at his athletic frame. I stared at the photo with a deeper interest than I cared to admit. For the first time, the idea of having a boyfriend seriously crossed my mind. I passed the phone back to her and watched as she put it in her bag.

"Do your parents know?" I asked curiously.

The response I got was an outburst of laughter from all the girls.

"If our parents knew about our boyfriends, we would be chained to the house. Actually, though, I think our *amma* knows. But she likes to be in denial," said Reshanthy.

"Yeah, they wouldn't like the idea of anything taking away our focus from our studies," Thurka pitched in.

They all nodded in agreement.

"I wish we could though," Selvi mused. "I mean it would be nice to not have to sneak around all the time."

I had never thought about what hiding a relationship from my parents would be like. "Isn't it exhausting? I mean what about summer holidays? How would you spend time with each other?"

Devi shrugged. "Mostly through talking on the phone or Skype. Sometimes we say we're going out with 'friends'. But that can be risky, since all our mothers know each other and can check up on us."

"Hmmm . . ." I said. I filed away the information in my head, just in case I might need it someday.

"What about you, Nisha?" Reshanthy asked.

I shook my head, "I've never had a boyfriend."

There was a collective "What?" and they all sat up. Their expressions showed they didn't believe me.

"No, come on, you're lying. You're way too pretty not to have a boyfriend." Reshanthy poked me, trying to get the truth out of me.

"Thank you for the compliment, Reshanthy." I smiled. "But no, I've never even gone on a date with a guy. I've just been focusing on school. And I'm too shy. Besides, I hardly go out, so I couldn't give the excuse of being with 'friends'. It's just always seemed more of a headache than it's worth."

"I know your parents are pretty strict," Thurka said sympathetically. "*Amma* always tells me they need to stop controlling everything you do."

Really? My parents were stricter than others? And their friends talked about it?

"So you don't like anyone at your school?" asked Selvi.

I fidgeted, not knowing whether I should answer that question. I didn't want to tell them about Todd. Especially because there was nothing to really tell. "Well . . . there are no Tamil guys I like at my school," I admitted.

I could tell that my inclusion of the word "Tamil" would lead them to ask the next obvious question. But before they could, the door opened. It was Keera Aunty bringing me my tea. As she handed the cup to me, she looked at the other girls. They had fallen silent and were all fussing with their clothes and phones. How much had Keera Aunty heard? I studied her face to see if there was any sign of disapproval, but she looked more tired than upset. Taking a sip of the milk tea, I closed my eyes for a brief second in appreciation. I let the flavour of the spices linger in my mouth before I opened my eyes.

"Thank you, Aunty, this is really good," I said sincerely with a smile.

She smiled in response, patting the top of my head before turning her attention to the rest of the group. "Food is ready. Go down and eat," Keera Aunty announced before leaving us.

We got up and made our way downstairs. I was more than grateful that I was saved from questions I didn't really know the answer to.

06 Dating by Any Other Name

THE NEXT FEW WEEKS brought some of the answers to those questions. As fate would have it, we had a new book report project that involved partners working very closely together. Mrs. Chou made everyone in the class pair up with the same people we had worked with for the first assignment. That meant Todd and I would be spending a lot of time together.

At first I was worried. What if we disagreed, or he was a bad partner? It would be awful if we couldn't work together to get a good enough grade. But I learned that I liked having Todd as a partner. He was hard working and extremely smart. Even better, he put a hundred percent into any work he did. He also understood the demands of my other courses. He gave me more time to work on my part of the report and offered to do more if things seemed too much for me. He also had a quirky sense of humour, and I often found myself laughing at his goofy expressions during our study sessions.

I was getting more and more comfortable with Todd. We started out as work partners, but soon we became friendlier, greeting each other with hugs and saying goodbye with the same. The more time we spent together, the more I felt free to be a person I hardly recognized . . . and the more confused I felt. My little high school crush was blossoming into something deeper, giving me the courage to dream of more.

It was a chilly Friday in early November. My parents had come home early from work. They were in the middle of what seemed to be a serious talk when I entered the living room. But they stopped talking and looked up at me. I stared back at them with a quizzical expression.

"What?" I asked.

"*Appa* bought *dosai*, it's in the fridge. Go eat. There's *sambar* and curry there too," my mother said. Then she turned back to my dad, "What kind of child is this? Going around with boys, especially at this age."

My dad nodded absently. He played with the remote as he gazed at the news on TV. I got the feeling he didn't want to continue the conversation now that I was home.

Not budging from my spot, I asked before my mother could say another word, "What happened?"

"It's Thurka. Keera Aunty found out that she has been seeing some guy. Now there is a big problem there. Keera Aunty called me to complain about it," my mother shared.

I paused a bit before speaking, "What's so bad about having a boyfriend?" I asked. "Didn't any of you guys have boyfriends or girlfriends when you were in school?"

My mother waved off my question. "We had crushes. But we wouldn't dare have a boyfriend. This boyfriend and girlfriend business is not part of our culture. A proper Tamil does not engage in such things."

"Okay. But aren't you and *Appa* a love marriage? I mean, to have a love marriage you need to, well . . . date to be able to fall in love . . ."

My father snorted a laugh, then he quickly stifled it, keeping his eyes glued to the TV. My mother didn't seem amused. "Your father and I." She glared at him before turning her attention back at me. "We liked each other. But we never dated. In fact, he did the honourable thing. He had his family come and asked my parents for my hand in marriage."

"But for *Appa* to feel confident to do that, you must have done something to give him some encouragement. You had to let him know that you liked him too," I persisted.

My mother placed a finger on her chin as she thought about it. "Yes, we talked a lot. And we got to know each other from that."

"Did you talk to each other with groups of other people around?" I asked her.

She shook her head. "No, it was just the two of us."

"So . . . what you're saying is, you and *Appa* dated."

She turned her glare on me. I couldn't see my father's expression as he avoided looking at his wife or me. But there was a slight smile at the corner of his lips that gave him away.

"Youngsters dating here is very different from how we interacted there," my mother let out.

"You like someone. And you're spending time alone with them on a regular basis with the goal of getting to know them and only them. That's dating. The process might be different here compared to how you 'dated' in Sri Lanka. But the concept is the same." I felt a slight rush as I challenged my mother. It felt good to make her question herself. I wanted to leave her speechless.

"Whatever it is, we made sure that whoever we liked was the person we were getting married to. Nowadays, Tamil kids can date one person one time and then switch to another person the next. *Aiyoo*! What type of shame will it bring to the family? People will think their daughter is a whore." My mother's face contorted into horror at the thought.

Shaking my head, I went into the kitchen and put food on a plate. The smell of the *dosai* and curry made my stomach rumble and my mouth watered in eagerness to eat my dinner. As I waited for the food to heat up in the microwave, my dad yelled to me, "Nisha, when is your deadline for university applications?"

I didn't answer right away. Was he going to start questioning me about it now? "Some time in the first week of December," I finally yelled back.

At the beep of the microwave, I took out my dinner. I made my way back to the living room and joined my parents on the couch.

"Have you already started looking at courses?" my dad asked.

I was glad my mouth was full, giving me time to shake my head and think of a good answer. "Not yet, I'm going to start tonight."

"Make sure you look into good science courses and the best medical schools in Canada. You want to be able get into a good medical school here. If we have to send you off to some other country to study, we will. But it's better if you plan from now to study here."

I kept eating my dinner so I did not have to speak as I thought about how to answer. Maybe if it took long enough, my father would not need an answer at all.

After I finished eating, I placed my plate on the coffee table. "Does that mean I get to choose what I want for myself?"

My father looked at me with a confused expression. "What?"

"You guys have chosen my courses for me all these years. And now you are telling me what programs and courses I should be looking at. Isn't it time I choose what I want to do for my future? What if I want to be something other than a doctor?" I felt myself starting to get nervous, even though I stared boldly at my parents.

"Like what?" My dad was clearly bewildered.

I shrugged, "I don't know. But I would like a chance to figure it out. You and Mom have always made decisions for me. I've started to see that it's actually a bit strange for someone my age to have all her decisions made for her by her parents. How do you expect me to grow up if you're not going to allow me to do things myself?" I looked away, too nervous to stare at them. Instead I focused my attention on the TV.

My father looked too shocked to speak. Finally, my mother said, "You're too young, you don't know what's good for you."

I felt a stab of disappointment at her response. I nodded. "Sure, if you say so." I got up and made my way to my room, walking with slouched shoulders and slow steps. The boldness I had felt just moments ago disappeared into blackness.

07 Jealousy

I WAS STILL DEEP IN THOUGHT over my university application and my parents' comments the next day. But I was startled back to reality when a pair of hands covered my eyes, dropping my sight into blackness. I could feel from the outline of the hands that the person behind me was male. I smiled to myself and said Todd's name. Still smiling, I turned to see his face, like a ray of sunshine on my gloomy thoughts.

"Hey, Todd, how's it going?"

"I'm doing good. You okay? You looked . . . upset," he said.

"Yeah. Yeah, I'm fine. Just drama with family," I responded. I tried to keep my voice light.

"Oh . . . what about?" His expression was curious as he looked at me.

"University and stuff. They want me to get into science and do pre-med. But I don't think it's what I want anymore. If I ever did." Worried about bringing down the mood, I asked, "Are you heading to class? Do you want to walk together?"

The sudden change in conversation helped. He nodded at me and the smile came back. I didn't want to give him a sad story and make him think I was "emo" or something.

"I was wondering, Nisha," Todd asked as we ambled down the hall, "are you free some time this week after school? I was hoping we could meet to put the finishing touches on our project."

I thought about my schedule and nodded. "In fact, I should be able to today," I replied. I would take any excuse to not head home right after school.

"Yeah, sure, today works."

As we reached my classroom, I turned to look at him. "Thanks for walking with me," I said shyly. I watched him fidget, thinking that he looked nervous, but why?

"No problem, my pleasure." Todd chuckled and scratched the back of his head. "So, today at three-thirty by the library?"

"Yep, see you."

As I watched him turn to walk away, someone yelled his name. I watched as a dark-haired girl ran up to him. It was Vanessa Persaud, a girl I knew from some of my classes. She threw her arms around Todd in a hug.

At first Todd seemed surprised at her actions. But within a few seconds he was returning her hug. Even when they separated, they smiled into each others' faces as they talked. Todd looked really happy to see her. Vanessa had her manicured hand on his arm and they were standing really close to each other.

A lump formed in my throat. I tried to stifle the jealousy that was ready to consume me. *Maybe that's her*, I thought to myself. Vanessa might be the girl Todd had said he liked. As I watched Vanessa pout her perfect pink-glossed lips at him, I felt nausea rise up in me.

Before I could turn and hurry away, I saw Todd turn in my direction. He caught me looking. I quickly looked away and scurried into the classroom. I took a seat just as the bell rang. I was left wondering how I was going to focus on my schoolwork for the rest of the day.

It was 3:15 by the time I made my way to my locker. I grabbed what I needed for the project with Todd: my copy of *Lord of the Flies*, my notes, and my laptop. As I made my way to the school library, my chest felt heavy. A part of me wanted to text Todd and tell him that I wasn't feeling well, that I had gone home. His interaction with Vanessa had left a sour taste in my mouth. I had never felt jealousy like this before, and

I didn't like it. But another part of me wanted to see him. I wanted to spend this last time alone with him before we handed in our project.

I saw Todd waiting by the door, his attention on his phone. I slowed my pace as I took a deep breath. I ordered myself to get my act together and to focus on the assignment. Todd must have heard my steps as I got closer to him. He looked up and smiled that smile that seemed to light up his face.

Giving him a half-smile back, I didn't even bother to say hi as I gestured him to enter the library. With a nod he walked in and I followed behind. We took a seat at an empty table and unpacked our notes and laptops without looking at each other. I opened up the file. The silence between us was awkward. I wanted nothing more than to sink under the table and hide.

"Do you think —"

"Which part —"

We both spoke together. Then we looked at each other for a few seconds before I gestured for him to go ahead.

Shaking his head, he said, "No, you go."

Okay, I thought, *I can do this*. "Do you think we need to add more about the symbolism? I feel like that part is too short." I turned my laptop to him so that he would be able to read what I had written.

"No, it's fine. Maybe you can give more examples so that it's more detailed."

Nodding, I started typing. We continued to sit in silence. We only spoke if we needed to change something or clarify what each of us was going to write. I would sneak glances at him as I worked, wondering if he was feeling the weirdness I was feeling. I wanted to break the silence but the image of him and Vanessa stopped me. I forced my attention back to the assignment.

As we were working, the librarian signalled to us that the library would close soon. I glanced at the time on my laptop and was surprised to learn we had been there for almost two hours.

"I don't have a printer. Do you?" Todd asked me.

I nodded as I packed up my bags.

"Then I'll send you my part. You can put it together with yours and print it out. If that's okay with you?"

"Sure no problem, " I agreed as I hitched my bag up on my shoulder.

I stood there, waiting for him to finish getting his things together, when his cell phone rang. He stared at his phone, looking hesitant to pick up.

I watched him as he continued to stare at the ringing phone. With a sigh, he swiped right and held the phone up to his ear. "Hello, Vanessa . . ." he said into the phone without looking at me.

I almost ran out of the library. But when I looked back, all I could see was Todd's confused face.

08 Close Becomes Closer

I HAD A SPARE ON THURSDAY AFTERNOONS. One busy Thursday I decided to spend the end of my day at the café near my school. It was a popular hangout for everyone in the area, especially students. It was a lot better than the dreary halls of the school. I had managed to avoid Todd for a few days while I tried to gather my emotions. I decided I was being silly for acting like a jealous, lovesick girl. He had told me he liked a South Asian girl and Vanessa was from West Indies. She wasn't

Tamil, so I wondered why he was reading my blog to gain insight. But whatever the case, I needed to stop overthinking what might or might not be happening with Todd. I had university applications to worry about.

I spent a few minutes browsing through the websites of universities in Ontario. I looked at all the programs and requirements. I was torn between courses on creative writing and the arts and the science-heavy programs I knew my parents were choosing for me. As much as they wanted me to study science and become a doctor, I found myself hating the idea. I mentally shuddered at the thought of spending four years of my life dedicated to something I had no interest in and no desire to do.

But I was no closer to figuring out what I wanted to do for myself. How could random arts courses lead me to the kind of career I was expected to have? With a sigh, I closed the university tabs and gave up trying to figure it out. If I didn't know what I wanted to do for myself, how could I complain about my parents' plan for me?

I sat back in my chair and looked around the café. There were only a handful of people there. Some were typing away on their laptops, completely focused. Others were grouped together, chatting away and sipping on their drinks. There was a couple by the corner who were seated at the same side of the table. They were holding hands, and the guy's other hand was draped around the girl's shoulder. Lips almost touching, they were whispering. And then their lips did touch and they were sharing a kiss. The guy looked to be Middle Eastern and the girl was East Asian. I smiled at their complete oblivion about where they were, at how their gaze was only on each other.

My smile turned into a frown as I caught sight of a middle-aged East Asian man sitting a few feet away from the couple. He occasionally looked at them, a look of disapproval etched deeply into his face. He was clearly bothered, either by seeing them as a couple or by their public display of affection.

I had grown up with the idea of marrying within my culture and it was rooted in my brain. But seeing mixed couples didn't surprise me. And I had to admit that I felt a bit envious that this boy and girl had the courage to challenge old-fashioned thinking. It made me wonder, if Todd and I were together, would we get looks like that, looks of disapproval or disgust? Worse, would my mom's Tamil friends gossip about me and call me a whore? I shook my head to try to get rid of the thought.

But the thought wouldn't go away. I had to write about it to explore how I really felt. Deciding to use the topic as one of my blog posts, I opened up a word document and started typing. I wanted to tackle all the stereotypes of being in a mixed relationship. I wanted to challenge the notion of moral superiority that came with marrying someone of one's own race. I wanted to take away the kind of thinking that was used as a crutch. It was a tool that allowed us to judge and treat each other unkindly.

Ideas were pouring out of my head and down to my fingers. I almost jumped out of my seat when I felt a hand tap my shoulder. There was Todd standing beside me. I quickly checked the time on the computer and was surprised to see it was 3:45 and school was out.

"Hey, you scared me," I said. I was a little annoyed that he had disturbed the flow of my writing.

"Yeah, I'm sorry. You looked like you were busy."

"Yeah, I was just getting something down while it was still fresh in my mind." As I spoke I saved the document to finish later.

"Can I sit here or do you want me to leave you alone?" he asked.

Nodding, I waved my hand to the seat across from me, "Go ahead."

"What are you working on?"

"Just writing something for my blog," I said without thinking. Then I froze when I realized what I had just revealed.

"You have a blog?" Todd sounded surprised. "How come you didn't tell me?"

I shrugged. "It's no big deal."

"That's totally a big deal. What's the blog called?" His voice was eager and I looked at him, trying to figure out if it was real. I hated myself for being cynical. But I didn't want to tell him too much, out of fear that I might let my guard down. I remembered how it felt to see him with Vanessa and knew that I had to control my feelings for Todd. But I wasn't going to lie.

"You actually know the blog already. It's *Confessions of a Sri Lankan Girl.*" I looked at Todd with my hands crossed in front of me, my expression as blank as I could make it.

Todd stared at me, mouth agape. "Seriously?" he asked after a while.

I simply nodded. I had to try hard to keep myself from smirking at his surprise.

Todd shook his head in wonder. "Wow! Why didn't you tell me when I wrote about it being one of my favourite blogs?"

"I dunno. Like I said, it's no big deal. And I don't really want the whole world to make the connection.

There are reasons my name isn't on the blog."

"I get that. But come on. I'm like . . . a fan. I'm kinda hurt that you didn't tell me."

I couldn't tell whether he was being serious. His face was solemn but there was a twinkle in his eye. I decided to play it off.

Cocking my head to the side, I pouted and gave him puppy dog eyes. "Awww, forgive me?"

A small laugh escaped from his lips. "Fine, I'll forgive you this time," he said. "I can't stay mad at you."

But after a brief pause he got serious again. "But maybe you're mad at me. How come you've been avoiding me for the past few days?"

Now it was my turn to be shocked. Was I that obvious in my attempt to squash my feelings for him? I opened my mouth, only to close it again. I cleared my throat and forced myself to lie. "I don't know . . . I don't know what you mean." Instead of coming out normal, my voice was a squeak. I felt my body grow hot in embarrassment as I saw a knowing smile spread across his face.

"Come on, Nisha. Every time I've tried to talk to you, you've basically run away."

"Well, I've been in a hurry."

He gave me an 'I don't believe you' look. I couldn't meet his eyes and looked away.

Seeing my composure crumble, Todd relented. His face melted into a gentle smile and he reached out and took my hand.

09 Seed of Rebellion

MY EYES WIDENED in shock and confusion. There I was, holding hands with the guy I had dreamed about for months. I couldn't do anything but stare at him.

Looking into my eyes, Todd gave my hand a gentle squeeze before he let go. I pulled my hand back quickly, but it was like I could still feel the warm pressure of his hand on mine. I was distracted by how good even the memory felt.

"I actually wanted to give you something," he

finally said. His voice was neutral, as if nothing had happened. As I tried to calm myself, I just stared as he pulled a piece of red paper from his bag and passed it to me.

I looked at the slightly crinkled paper, reading the big bold letters printed on it.

Green Tree Publishing is currently looking for emerging diverse writers for an upcoming publication. We invite interested unpublished writers to submit a short piece (up to 15,000 words) to rparekh@greentreepublishing.com.

"I came across this when I went to the library over the weekend," he said. "I thought of you right away. I would have given this to you sooner, but you were too busy running away from me," he added wryly.

I gave him a guilty smile. I looked back at the paper, unable to say anything. The fact that he had thought of me caught me off guard. It left my heart feeling full with a mixture of wonder and gratitude.

Even more touching was that he believed that I could do this . . . that my writing was good enough to be in a book. I felt a lump form in my throat and my eyes grew misty to the point where the words on the paper became a blur.

Quickly blinking away the tears, I gave him a wobbly smile. All I could get out was a whispered thank you. I desperately wanted to regain my calm.

Todd must have seen my watery eyes, as his expression grew concerned. "Hey . . . I didn't mean to upset you. I mean, I thought you would like the idea but —"

Shaking my head violently, I interrupted him, "No, no." I cleared my throat. "I'm not upset about it. I'm actually really touched. Thank you." I got up off my seat and stretched out my arms.

He got up and we hugged each other. Although it only lasted a few seconds, the hug felt like it went on much longer.

We broke apart and I looked up at him. I let the happiness that I felt show through my eyes. His hand cupped my face, wiping away the tear that had escaped down my cheek. He gave me a tender kiss on my forehead.

"No problem at all," he whispered to me. "You can do this, Nisha. You should do this. Something for you . . . that makes you happy."

As I nodded, I knew I had a deeper connection to him than I had ever felt before. I knew that he felt it too. I could see we were drawing a few stares from the other patrons our way. Not wanting to reveal my feelings in public, I broke away and took a seat back on the chair.

Todd was still standing as his phone buzzed in his jacket pocket. He took it out, looked at it and then put it back. "I have to go. My mom needs me to pick up some groceries," he said quietly. He held out his hand to me and I clasped it. Giving it a squeeze he gave me a half smile. "I'll see you tomorrow?"

I bobbed my head in agreement and he left. I sat there, staring after him.

"Nisha, have you thought about university?" my father asked from his seat at the dining table. He was doing something on his laptop.

"Mmhmm," was all I could say in response. I was watching TV, focused on the news.

"When are you planning on applying? It's almost the end of October. Is the deadline coming up soon?"

My mother was walking around upstairs. I could hear the bathroom taps turning on and off as she cleaned up. It was a cool Sunday night and I felt too lazy to go out. Instead, I chose to listen to my father try to plan my future.

I didn't answer him. Instead, I continued staring at the TV, using the time to think of what to say to him. I had spent the last few days looking at different courses and schools online. But I still had no idea what to take. Nothing seemed likely to both appeal to me and get my parents' approval.

Out of sheer frustration, I had gone to see Mr.

Gilford, my school's guidance counsellor. When I asked him for advice, he suggested that I take an array of courses to find out which ones piqued my interest. He said that lots of students found their area of study and chose their majors after starting undergraduate work. I had never thought that way about my studies. My parents believed in setting a goal and then spending years achieving it. Learning that my indecision was pretty normal was a huge relief. I started to look at which universities I would be interested in attending with this in mind. But I hadn't actually applied anywhere yet.

"Nisha!" my dad called out.

I whipped my head in his direction. He sat there, looking at me, expecting an answer.

"Sorry, *Appa*. What did you say?" I pretended I hadn't heard him. Maybe it would stop him from giving me a lecture on not paying attention. Would he insist I get my hearing checked if he thought I was going deaf?

His face showed he was annoyed. "You should be doing this! I'm not the one going to university. Your deadline is coming up, and you're just sitting there, watching television like a couch potato," he scolded.

I lowered the TV volume with the remote. I might as well keep feigning deafness. I got up and made my way towards my dad. "Sorry, *Appa*. What did you say?" I asked again.

"Have you thought about university and med school?" He spoke slowly, as if talking to a child.

"Yeah, I was thinking of McMaster University or the University of Toronto. They have good programs. I thought I might start there."

His eyes lit up as he turned back to his laptop. He started clicking away as I peered at his screen in curiosity. He was browsing university websites, clicking link after link in fervid interest. "I think you need to apply to schools with a top medical program first. Doing well in science courses there will increase your chances of getting into their medical school."

I looked at the website. Why couldn't I make myself feel the excitement he clearly had for my future in medicine? "Yeah . . ." I said, staring blankly at the screen. "I was looking into those schools as well as McGill."

My father's face lit up again. "What program? Biology, Biochemistry? You should take sciences that will help you do well when you go to med school. I mean you don't —"

"Actually, *Appa*, I was thinking of just applying as undecided. I can figure out what I want to do later on." Interrupting him probably wasn't a good idea. But I had to let him know that my plans didn't exactly match his.

By this time my mother had made her way downstairs. She stopped in front of my father and me. She was too surprised to even scold me for interrupting my father. There were a few moments of silence. I could feel my heart thudding. Sweat from nervousness and fear made my palms feel clammy.

10 *Fighting Back*

"WHAT DO YOU MEAN 'UNDECIDED'?" My dad finally spoke, his voice quiet and low. A shiver of fear filled me for a moment. Memories of my parents whipping me with a hanger for disobeying them came flooding into my mind. The South Asian version of spanking was a lot more painful than a simple smack on the butt from a parent's hand.

But I knew I needed to do this. If I didn't speak up now, I would forever be stuck with someone else's idea of what my life should be. It was mental slavery. The more I felt and saw it, the more I felt the need to fight back. Swallowing the fear, I somehow found my voice. "I spoke to the guidance counsellor. He said that schools will allow students to be undecided for the first two years. That way they can take different courses to help decide what they want to specialize in."

I looked at my parents. I didn't know whether to be grateful or fearful of their silence. My father turned to look at my mother and then he looked back at me. I was surprised to see the raised eyebrows and the lack of expression on his face. I thought my mind must have been playing tricks on me. Or he was trying to fool me by hiding his anger. My mother's expression showed just as little emotion as she continued to stare at me.

My dad opened his mouth to speak. But it was my mother who spoke first. "So, you're going to be sitting in class wondering what to do? You are going to waste time and money on useless things and then have to make up the courses you need?"

I looked at her, wondering what she was talking about. She pulled out a carefully folded piece of red paper. It looked familiar. My heart sank when I realized what it was. It was the notice that Todd had given me.

"I found this paper in your bag, Nisha. What is this? Did your teacher put you up to this?" She angrily shook the paper in the air.

I shook my head. "No, it's just something I found. And since I write —"

"What do you mean you write? What do you write?" my father demanded. He reached out his hand for the paper and my mother let him take it.

"N-Nothing. Just a b-blog about growing up Sri Lankan." I couldn't keep my voice from breaking.

My father looked at the paper. Then he crumpled it angrily and threw it away.

"I knew I shouldn't have allowed you to take that stupid Writing class," my mother said. Her voice was full of disgust. "Stupid things like that take you away from your studies."

"Show me this blog," demanded my father. He jerked the laptop to face me.

My hands were slightly shaking. Holding back a sob, I typed the web address into the browser and slowly turned the laptop back to him. My mother walked up to stand next to him to read. I quickly took a few steps back to create some distance between my furious parents and me.

They didn't even read my writing. They just looked through the blog titles. I could imagine what they were thinking. I had written on topics like feminism in Tamil culture, the issue of skin colour, sexual abuse, and interracial dating. I shuddered to think what was going through their minds. They probably didn't think their proper, innocent daughter even thought of those things, or knew those words.

My father suddenly slammed the laptop closed and pointed at it. "Is this how you show your culture to the rest of the world?" he bit out. "You write about this garbage and give our heritage a bad name."

"You didn't even read anything I wrote. How can you say it's garbage?" I exclaimed.

"You write about interracial dating and other nonsense. What are you trying to do, give yourself a bad name?" he asked in an accusing tone. "Give us a bad name?"

"No! No one knows it's me. Writing what I think and feel is something I do from time to time. And I'm good at it." I started to feel the first flicker of anger. How dare they accuse me without actually reading what I wrote?

"Do you have a boyfriend or something? A non-Tamil boyfriend? Is that why you're writing this crap? To make excuses for behaving shamefully?"

"No!" I was almost screaming. "I write because it makes me happy. It's the only thing that makes me feel like I am myself. It makes me feel free when you both try to take my freedom away." Rage filled me. I felt ready to explode.

"I have done EVERYTHING you ever asked me to," I continued. "I have focused on my studies and nothing else. I've given up any friends and social time I could have because I wanted to do well for you both. But instead of supporting me in this one thing that actually makes ME happy, you accuse me of doing it just to cause you some kind of shame?" By this time I was actually screaming.

I saw the look on both their faces freeze in shock at my outburst. I didn't care anymore. I had tasted freedom with Todd. After being able to be myself, going back to this constant pressure was not something I was willing to do.

"You." I pointed my finger angrily at my father. "You want me to have a secure future? How exactly do you expect that to happen when I have lived my whole life following decisions other people have made for me? How can I make a good future if I've never done any thinking for myself?"

My parents stared at me, speechless. The shock and anger were gone from their faces. They looked at me like I was a stranger. I went to pick up the paper that my dad had thrown away and I stomped out of the room. I ran to my room and slammed the door shut behind me.

The sudden surge of rage left as quickly as it came. The tears I had held back suddenly emerged. Soon I was sliding to the floor, sobs wracking my whole body. I crawled into bed and curled on my side. The tears still flowed freely down my face and drenched the pillow. What had I done?

11 Secret Lair

I CLICKED THE "SEND" BUTTON. I let out a deep breath I didn't know I had been holding. It was 5:30 on a Wednesday, two days before the deadline posted on the call for submissions that Todd had given to me. I gave myself a mental pat on the back for sending in my writing early. It had taken me more than two weeks. I had spent days trying to figure out what to send in. Then I decided to write a new piece. It was a short story about a girl who had lived her whole life being obedient and who finally becomes empowered enough to express herself.

Todd sat across the library table from me, his head buried in a book. When he heard me stop typing, he lifted his head to look at me. "Done?" he mouthed. I nodded. His mouth widened into the biggest smile as he got up to sit next to me. His arm stretched out to give me a tight hug and he kissed me quickly on my forehead.

"Congratulations. I'm so proud of you," he whispered to me.

My body melted against his. I sighed thinking of how perfect the moment was. But perfect moments can't last forever. I knew we had to be careful about kissing in public. Breaking away slightly, I asked, "Do you want to read it?"

He shook his head. "Nope, I will read it when it gets published." His voice sounded more confident than I felt.

I giggled. "Silly, what if they don't choose me? There is no guarantee."

His expression was serious as he looked straight into my eyes. "They will. I have faith."

I was in awe of his conviction. My heart fluttered and I looked away. A whole mix of emotions filled me, tightening my throat.

I leaned back into his arms and closed my eyes. We both sat in silence as his hand caressed my shoulder. I sat there, looking at the people around me, but not really paying attention. Instead, I was focused on my feelings for Todd. There was no question I was falling for him. But being with him like this confused me. Part of me wanted to believe he had feelings for me. It certainly seemed that way. He showed it through his actions, if not his words. But I didn't want to assume feelings that weren't real, or come off as being desperate. I had never interacted on a deep level with any boy, let alone a boy outside of my own culture. Even a secret boyfriend would be safe if he was a Tamil guy. He would know the culture, what we would have to hide and how. But Todd had no idea. I had no idea of how to teach him. And I felt like that was driving me insane.

I felt Todd gently shake me. "Hey, do you have to go home right away?" he asked.

I thought about my parents and how we still weren't speaking. I shook my head.

"Do you want to go somewhere with me?" Todd's voice was strangely shy.

"Sure," I answered as I straightened up. "Where are we going?"

"It's a secret place. Nothing fancy, but it's special to me. I like to go there by myself when I need to check out. I think you'll like it too."

"Is it walking distance, or do we need to drive?" I started packing my belongings.

"We need to go out of the city. It's not in the suburbs, more like the country. We can take my car."

Mixed in with curiosity and confusion, I felt a flutter of excitement in my stomach. The thought of Todd and me being completely alone brought wild thoughts to my imagination. I felt a longing stir within me. "Get a grip," I muttered to myself as we headed out the door. The setting sun had turned the sky a colourful array of magenta, red, and orange mixed into the blue. It was as vivid as what I was feeling inside.

We walked towards his car, a black Honda Civic. Despite a few scratches, the car looked well taken care of. I got into the passenger seat and quickly looked around. There was no litter inside the car, no food wrappers or pieces of paper needing to be recycled. The fabric of the seat I was in was slightly worn with a few holes, but it was clean. As Todd got in, I asked, "Todd, are you a neat freak?"

"Why do you ask?" He started the engine. The car sputtered before coming to life. He carefully looked back and put the car in reverse.

"Because this is an old car. But there's no dust, not a single spot of rust."

He laughed. "I don't have money to spend on a new car. So I try to keep what I have in good condition."

"Fair enough. Did your parents get this for you as a gift or something?"

"No, I've worked since I was fifteen to save up to buy this car. This was the best I could afford."

"How much did you pay for it?"

"A thousand. I got it off an uncle who was upgrading. He took pity on me and dropped the price a bit."

"Why didn't you ask your parents for a little more money to get something better?"

Todd paused. The longer his silence, the more I thought he wasn't going to answer. But then he started to speak again. "My parents aren't rich. My dad worked in construction before he had a workplace accident. Now he's on disability. My mom works as a personal support worker. But that doesn't pay much, so my parents couldn't afford to give me extra cash for anything not essential."

"Oh." It was all I could say in response. I processed what he had just told me, and the fact that he had revealed it to me. I thought about my parents. We weren't swimming in money, but we did live very comfortably. I never knew them to worry about paying any bills. "So you work to support your family?"

He nodded. "Whenever they need me to. I usually try to save more than I spend, just in case my family needs some emergency cash."

"Hmmm . . ." was all I could say as I turned to look out the window.

We sat in silence after that. But it wasn't awkward. Todd didn't seem ashamed by what he had shared with me. The soft jazz music playing in the car seemed to set a calm, tender mood. But I stared out the window. I focused my attention on the passing scenery so I wouldn't be overcome with nervousness. When Todd and I were together, it was in a public place. I was always able to keep myself in check out of fear of other people watching. But now, I was terrified that I was going to do something stupid and embarrass myself.

There were fewer and fewer houses the longer we drove. Empty fields and trees overtook my vision. Streetlights disappeared and the sun slowly sank us into darkness. The only light visible was the one from the car's headlights, shining into the darkness ahead of the car.

After about twenty minutes, Todd pulled onto a dirt road. At the end of it sat a beat-up looking house with shuttered windows. The roof looked like it was falling in, just like the battered walls. "This is your escape?" I asked.

"Not unless I'm looking for inspiration for a horror movie," he said with a smile.

I stared at him wide-eyed. He looked at me and chuckled. "Relax, silly. Where we're going is behind the house."

That didn't sound a whole lot better. But as Todd slowly drove the car around the house, I could make out something in the dim light. It was shaped like a house, only smaller than any house I had seen. As the car headlights hit it, I realized it was a shed. Unlike the house, the shed was in excellent condition. It had recently been painted a dark brown and the roof was patched but intact. A small window with a white sill and trim was on the side of the shed. The white door seemed to shine in welcome.

"Welcome to my humble abode!" he exclaimed.

12 More than Friends

MY CURIOSITY GREW as I got out of the car and followed Todd. I was surprised to see a padlock on the door. I heard keys jingling as Todd got out a ring crammed with keys. He fiddled with the lock before finding the right key and opening the door. He walked in and flicked the light switch.

Suddenly the space was filled in a soft glowing light. It revealed a large beanbag chair in the corner with a rug worn soft in front of it. There was a small, white shelf beside it with a selection of books. Opposite the beanbag was a loveseat that had clearly seen better days. It sagged and the fabric was thin in places. But it was clean and looked surprisingly comfortable. There was also a small wooden table against the wall. On it I could see Styrofoam cups, a kettle and two unmarked containers. Knowing Todd's habits, I assumed the containers held tea bags and sugar.

Despite the worn furniture there was something warm and cozy about the place. I walked in further, heading towards the bookshelf. I ran my fingers over the line of books. The titles were a mix of fiction and non-fiction. I pulled out a book that looked familiar and analyzed it front and back. It was *A Thousand Splendid Suns* by Khaled Hosseini, one of my favourites. I looked up to find Todd watching my every move, my every reaction.

"Have you read Hosseini's other book, *The Kite Runner?*" I asked.

Todd shook his head. "No, not yet. I'm currently

reading *The Book of Negroes*. Have you heard of it?"

"Yeah, I have, it's the one by Lawrence Hill. I read it, and watched the TV version too. The book is better."

I put the Hosseini book back on the shelf and picked out another one. *The Girl on the Train*. I turned it over to read the back cover and the description caught my curiosity. I took the book with me as I plopped myself on the loveseat. *I was right, it is comfortable*, I thought as I skimmed through the pages of the book.

"This looks good," I said, holding it up.

"I haven't read it yet. My aunt gave it to me last Christmas," Todd said as he took a seat next to me.

I placed the book on my lap and gave the room another look over. "So are we trespassing?"

He chuckled, "Not at all. This whole place is my uncle's. He has no use for it because he's a truck driver and is on the road a lot. So he lets me use it whenever I want to just be."

"Why doesn't he just sell it if he has no use for it?"

"I dunno. Maybe he has plans for it in the future." Todd shrugged. "But I'm not going to question him about it and give him ideas. Otherwise I might have to give this up."

"How often do you come here?" I asked curiously.

"Whenever the worries at home get too much. We live in a small, cramped house and there is not a lot of privacy. So I like to come here to read or do homework, or just to get away." He looked around. "I've come to really need this place. It grounds me."

Despite the fact that the shed was so isolated, I could feel something special and warm here. It was Todd's escape from the outside world. It let me look inward too. The easy silence allowed me to focus on me, what I wanted, instead of what the outside world wanted.

I felt a tingling sensation trail from my head to my neck as Todd played with my hair. I glanced back at him. He looked pensive as he stared into space.

I gently nudged him. "You okay?" I asked.

He looked at me, his eyes moving to my lips and then back to my eyes. I swallowed hard, trying to keep my thoughts rational. As I bit my lip, I saw a flash of desire in his eyes. I couldn't move or break my eyes away. I felt myself drowning in his stare.

Todd's face inched closer to mine. My hands, which had been resting on his chest, clutched his shirt. I pulled him towards me and our lips met. I had never felt anything like this before. A feeling that was equal parts desire and shock consumed me. It was as if someone else had taken over my body and I was unable to control anything.

It was Todd who pulled away. For a moment I was left dazed, as if I had just woken up abruptly from a dream.

"Nisha, we should stop." His voice sounded like he was struggling to speak. He was pushing me away, but his hand refused to release its hold on the back of my neck.

"Oh hell —" he let out suddenly. He pulled me closer. He kissed me again, this time with a passion that was like something out of a steamy romance novel.

Then, just as quickly, he pulled away again. "Okay, we have to stop. I don't want to do this like this."

Still dazed, I stared at him, "I'm sorry T —"

He shook his head as if trying to shake the sense back into it. "No! Don't apologize, I'm the one who should apologize."

I must have looked very confused. He held my hand, his eyes earnest. "Nisha, when I brought you here I wanted to ask you out. That's all. I just wanted to give you the chance to say yes or no. I didn't mean to kiss you like that. I'm sorry."

"You wanted to ask me out? Why couldn't you do that at the café?" I was puzzled.

"Because I wanted it to be special. It's corny, I know. But I was hoping that by bringing you here you could see how special you are to me."

I sucked in a deep breath. Here was the guy I had dreamed of for all of these years asking me out. I didn't know what to say. "Why don't you ask me now?"

He smiled at me. "Nisha, will you go out with me? I would like to take you out on a proper date."

I giggled, and gave him a peck on the lips. "Of course I'll say yes! Todd, I've had a crush on you for so long."

"You have?" As I nodded, he said, "Damn I wish I had known sooner. I noticed you years ago. I've wanted to ask you out forever."

"Then why didn't you say anything?" I asked.

"I didn't think you would go out with me. You were so serious about school and I knew you never dated. Every time I tried to work up the courage to talk to you, I chickened out. Then we started working together on the project. And there we were talking to each other. You turned out to be as great as I thought you might be. So I finally decided to grow a pair and ask you."

I laughed at the irony of it all. As we hugged each other, my heart felt ready to explode with happiness. Even though it was night and the sky was dark, the whole world suddenly seemed brighter.

13 Doubt Settles In

AFTER TODD AND I KISSED, I went from feeling on cloud nine to being a nervous wreck.

I woke up early the next morning, eager to see Todd. I wore a smile and walked with a slight skip in my step as I held on to the memory of the night before. I reached for my phone to text him, but then I stopped myself. *Would it be wrong to contact him first? Would I come off as clingy?* I thought, as fear of seeming desperate held me back.

At school, Todd was nowhere to be found. Concern gnawed at me. But I fought the temptation to text him. I waited until the next day. I would talk to him in person. But when I saw him from afar, he was with two other guys. Todd's head was down while the guy on his right chatted away. I stared at him, willing him to look up at me. My heart was racing with excitement. A part of me longed to just run up to him and greet him with a hug. Unable to contain myself, I shouted, "Todd!" and got his attention.

Todd smiled and gave a quick wave. I returned the smile, my eyes hopeful as I waved back at him. He continued walking my way, but the happiness I was feeling slowly faded. It dawned on me that he wasn't coming to me, but was going to walk past me. With a final fleeting glance and smile, he turned away, walking down the school hall with his friends.

I stood, utterly confused. Then a rush of shame and pain overtook me. I gasped, trying to catch my breath. But it seemed to have escaped me. I fell back against the wall. I felt a touch on my shoulder and I turned to numbly look at the concerned eyes of the girl beside me. She was speaking to me, but her voice sounded like it was coming from far away. After a few minutes I stood up straight, forcing myself to gather my wits. I had to get out of there.

"Hey?" I finally felt the gentle shake of her hands on my shoulders. "You okay?"

Focusing my eyes on her, I was able to quickly mutter, "Yes I'm . . . just not feeling well." I quickly closed my locker and scurried to the bathroom.

I locked myself in one of the stalls and leaned against the door. Tears streamed down my face. In my mind I told myself I was a stupid fool over and over again. I didn't know what to expect after Todd and I spilled out our feelings to each other, but it certainly wasn't this. *What did you expect, Todd to come to school with a bouquet of flowers?* I thought. I tried to be rational. We just had one kiss. And now I was flipping out over him not stopping to say hi. Although my mind tried to make sense of his behaviour, my heart was left in complete confusion. I had no experience with boys and had no way of knowing where we stood. At that moment, I hated myself for confessing my feelings for him. I made a vow to not let what he had done affect me anymore.

For the rest of the day, and the day after, I did my best to ignore the fact that Todd clearly had no interest in talking to me. Even during the classes we had together, I made it a point to sit as far away from him as the seating plan allowed. I caught him looking at me a few times, and when I couldn't keep our eyes from meeting, he smiled. But was that confusion filling his eyes too? I tried to smile before quickly looking away and distracting myself with whatever the teacher was saying at the front of the class. I held on to my icy cool expression as a smokescreen to hide the fear and hurt I was feeling inside.

During this time, I spent evenings hiding away in my room. I tried to bury my thoughts in studying. The one time I spent in the company of my parents in the living room, I couldn't focus on the news broadcast on TV. I let my mind wander to thoughts about Todd and, for a moment, I allowed the sadness and the longing to consume me. The feelings got more and more intense. This was dangerous. I shook my head and glanced at my parents. They were giving each other a look before they turned their gaze towards me. Clenching my jaw as I let out a deep breath, I quickly stood and made my way to my room before any questions were asked. I found myself often watching my phone. My heart skipped a beat every time it buzzed, only to plummet into despair as I realized there was no text from Todd.

By the weekend, I was carrying around a heavy feeling in my chest all day. I realized that I needed to talk to Todd. I couldn't carry on like this, my mind filled with doubts and questions. But how could I do that? I had left it too long to just call him. Besides, I was as afraid of what he might say as of the chance he might not even answer.

I decided to spend my Saturday in the library. Maybe the change of environment would provide some relief from the pain gnawing at my brain and heart. I grabbed my laptop and made my way downstairs. My parents were sitting in the living room drinking their late morning tea. My relationship with them had broken down, now consisting only of short answer questions and a clipped yes or no.

Not wanting to feel worse than I already did, I didn't say a word to them as I left the house. I decided to walk the fifteen minutes to the library, thinking the scenery mixed with the cold air would at least let me feel like I could breathe. The crisp air caressed my face as I huddled deeper into my jacket. There was something about the coldness that seemed to freeze my hurting heart, briefly easing the pain. As I neared the library, I thought I might stay outside longer until my thoughts and feelings were completely frozen. But I had schoolwork to do and I was behind on my blog posts. I spent a few hours in the library, trying to distract myself, filling my time with writing. But when I tried to type, my feelings for Todd would emerge and I found myself writing the same circular questions that filled my head. After a while I gave up on writing altogether. Instead I put all my energy into looking at different university programs. I was surprised that thoughts of my future could interest me. I narrowed down my choices to my top five. The deadline was in a month and I had to make the decision soon.

14 Wedding Romance

SOMEONE WAS SHAKING ME, taking me away from the comforting blanket of sleep. I groaned, unwilling to open my eyes. I writhed in protest of the intrusion into my slumber. The hand continued to shake, more aggressively now, and I heard a voice in the distance telling me to wake up. As I slowly started to become conscious, I realized that the voice was in fact right beside me. I opened my eyes halfway to see my mom standing beside my bed.

"Wake up, Nisha. You need to get ready for the wedding," she said.

"What wedding?" I croaked out.

"Remember? Mala Aunty's daughter is getting married today. I told you about this months ago." My mom stood there with a cup in her hand. "Drink your tea. It will help you wake up," she instructed as she placed the cup on my night table.

I stared blankly at the steaming tea for a few seconds. Then I reached out to my charging phone beside it. It was 5:00 a.m. I let out another loud groan and pulled the covers over my head, telling my body to go back to sleep.

"No, no, no. Come on, wake up," Mom said, pulling the covers away from me. "Drink your tea, it will help you wake up," she repeated as she walked out of my room.

I let out a cry of frustration. I struggled to sit up, my eyes still half closed. I cupped the tea in my hands. Taking smalls sips, I willed the caffeine to infuse some energy into my body. I realized I had a vague memory of my mother speaking about the wedding months ago. But I hated going to weddings. I had pretended that not listening meant I somehow didn't have to attend. It didn't work.

Once I finished my tea, I got out of bed. My body protested, but I forced myself to walk to the bathroom. After I showered, I felt more awake. I was as ready as I ever would be for the ordeal.

I came back into my room to find a turquoise coloured *saree* on my bed. I didn't recognize it, but I knew it must be from the stash of *sarees* my mom had acquired for me over the years. I put on the blouse and skirt, leaving the long wrap on the bed. Then I applied my makeup and styled my hair.

My mom came into my room, dressed and ready to go. "Are you done?" she asked.

"I need you to help me wear this," I said as I applied the final coating of mascara.

She nodded and left my room, only to come back a minute later with a small container of hair pins. They would hold the *saree* in place.

She wrapped the *saree* around me skilfully. Then she secured it with the pins, making sure that I was able to walk in it comfortably. As she was doing so, I adorned my neck, ears, and wrists with gold-plated jewellery. I looked at myself in the mirror and my mom stepped back to take a look at the results of our work. "You look beautiful," she said.

I looked back at the mirror. The turquoise of the *saree* and the gold of the jewellery complimented my wheat-coloured skin. My eye makeup was a dramatic mix of gold with a hint of green and turquoise. My lipstick made my mouth red and pouty. I smiled and turned around, admiring myself. I couldn't help it, but I wished Todd could see me like this.

I grabbed my clutch and headed downstairs. My dad was ready and waiting on the couch, flipping through TV channels. My mom rummaged through her shoes to find something that would match her own *saree*.

As my father drove to the venue, I sat in the back seat and stared aimlessly at the passing scenery. My thoughts drifted to Todd. I felt a pang in my chest and my hands turned into fists. A flicker of anger sparked within me. How could I be falling for someone who didn't care about me the same way? Mixed with hurt, the anger slowly spread through my body. I closed my eyes and took in a deep breath, my jaws clenching as I fought not to think about him. I bit my lip hard, allowing the pain to distract me. It was far too early for me to be up on a weekend morning. But part of me was grateful for the distraction, as it would help keep me away from thoughts of Todd.

As we pulled in to the gates of the hall, I could see a large group of people gathered by the doors. The sound of the *thavil nadeswaram*, the windpipe and barrel-shaped drums that played during Hindu wedding ceremonies, suddenly blasted. They signalled the arrival of the groom.

My parents and I slowly made our way to the doors, part of an entourage of colourful *sarees* and *kurthas*. The groom was welcomed into the elaborately decorated hall and led towards the altar where the wedding rituals would take place. To my surprise there were already a lot of people in the hall. With the addition of the crowd we were a part of, the number of guests could easily be a thousand.

I trailed behind my parents as they walked around, trying to find someone that they knew. My mom caught sight of someone and waved her hand in their direction. Then she pulled my dad and me to follow her. We squeezed through a maze of tables and chairs surrounded by the sound of excited chattering. I saw Keera Aunty and Kumar Uncle sitting at the table we were heading towards. I waved at them and smiled as we made our way to them. When we finally got to the table, I took a seat beside my mother and looked around. South Asians seemed to crave extravagance when it came to weddings. Having gone to what seemed like hundreds of them, the celebration no longer held any interest or excitement for me. I wished I could spend those precious weekend hours in bed sleeping instead. But any time I tried to get out of it, my protests were met with deaf ears. My parents wouldn't take no for an answer. I had to attend.

"It's good way to show off your future marriage potential," my mother had once said.

I remember being repulsed at the thought of getting married, or even the thought of boys. But I had learned early that weddings were a time for parents to market their sons and daughters. Every wedding held the seeds of weddings to come.

Letting out a deep sigh, I allowed my focus to turn to the altar. The priest was chanting a prayer. He sounded a bell as he lit the sacred fire and moved it in a circle around the bride and groom. The couple sat rigid, their eyes following the priest as he conducted the prayer. The bride's face was covered by a veil so I couldn't see her expression. I could see the groom shooting shy glances her way. I couldn't help but smile.

I had never really thought of having a boyfriend. Beyond my crush with Todd, I never allowed myself to stick on thoughts of being alone with a guy, let alone being kissed by one. My early daydreams of Todd were no more than that, daydreams. But after the night at the shed, I was left actually yearning for him. My body longed to be held by him. I wanted to feel his breath on my face as his arms wrapped around me. I wanted to taste his lips again. I had discovered something new, and I didn't want to go back to my quiet, obedient life.

15 All That Glitter and No Gold

THE WEDDING CONTINUED into the second phase. The bride was gently led out of the hall to change into the *koorai saree*. The groom's hands were clutched in front of him, and I could see his eyes focus on the door his bride had left through. Another man was talking to him, but the weak nods he responded with made it clear that his mind was focused on his bride to be. For the first time, I actually felt happy at a wedding. I was glad to witness this union because I finally understood what someone in love must feel.

The pause in the ceremony gave guests the chance to walk around. They mingled with relatives and friends as they waited for the bride to come back. A few people who knew my parents came by our table. As my parents introduced me as their daughter, I could see these strangers taking in my appearance. Approval showed in their smiles. I felt uncomfortable, but knew I had to be polite. I gave each of them a small smile of acknowledgement.

A middle-aged woman dressed in a tacky *saree* came by our table. "Indra, good god it's been a long time," she gushed. My mom let out a scream of excitement and laughed as she hugged the woman. She turned to all of us and said, "This is Sothy. We studied nursing together back in Jaffna."

"We go waaayyy back when," Sothy said as they hugged each other again.

My mom turned her old friend towards me. "This is my daughter, Nisha," she said. Sothy looked at me and smiled as if she was assessing an item she was about to buy. Instead of greeting me, she turned back to my mom, "Very pretty," she said. Only then did she address me. "You know, my son is here too, I will bring him over later on and introduce him." *Good lord,* I thought, *can she be any more obvious?*

Suddenly, I couldn't take it anymore. My parents were parading me around, and their friends were treating me like something that could be bought and sold. I excused myself to go to the washroom. I felt like running away, but I couldn't do that to my parents. A few minutes later I exited the washroom, but I wasn't ready to return to the table. I leaned on the doorframe at the entrance of the dining hall, watching the wedding guests mill around. I saw Sothy Aunty walking my way and smiling. *Maybe she is heading for the washroom I just left?* I smiled back politely, hoping she would pass by me. To my dismay she stopped in front of me.

"Hi!" she said. Her voice was eager, too eager for my taste.

"Uhh, hello," I responded.

"Are you enjoying yourself?"

I nodded. "Yeah, it's nice. A bit too much, but nice."

"They did a great job with the decorations." She waved a hand at the room. "I really love the colour choice. Very elegant."

I nodded again.

She put a hand on my arm. But instead of a light touch, it was like a vice grip. I couldn't get away from her. "My son is over there," she said brightly. "Come, I'll introduce you two."

Before I could say no thank you, she pulled me towards a guy in a grey suit standing by the bar. He was tall, with thick, well-styled black hair and a goatee. He had light brown skin, broad shoulders, and an athletic frame. By any standard, he would be considered a perfect example of a South Asian hottie. He flashed a confident smile my way as he watched his mom pretty much drag me to him. I saw a gleam of interest in his eyes as he took a sip of his drink. I felt discomfort and shyness overtake me as I stood before him awkwardly.

"Theeban, this is Nisha. Nisha's mom and I go way back in Sri Lanka. We both studied nursing together." Sothy Aunty presented me like a gift to her son.

With a stiff smile I looked at him. I turned to his mother and then back to him, not knowing what to do.

"Hello," Theeban said as he held out his hand to me. I looked at it for a second, as if I didn't know what it was. Then I quickly shook it. I was surprised when he held on longer than was comfortable. I tried to release my hand from his.

"I'm going to leave you two to talk," said Sothy Aunty, looking at our locked hands. With a grin she went off before I could stop her.

What was I supposed to say to this guy? "So . . . um . . . what grade are you in?" I asked.

Theeban let out a laugh. "I'm not in any grade, I'm in my second year of university."

"Oh cool, what are you taking?"

"Biochemistry at Guelph."

"Oh that's nice. You want to become a doctor?"

Theeban shrugged. "That's the plan if I get into a

med school here. If not, I'll have to see if I can get in overseas. What about you?"

We started walking away from the bar and made our way outside. The cold air sent a sudden shiver down my body. Along with getting away from the crush of people, it shook me out of the daze I had been in all day.

Completely ignoring his question, I asked, "Is becoming a doctor what you want? Or are you doing it because of your family?"

He shrugged again. "Good profession, good money. It comes with prestige . . ." he trailed off.

I didn't say anything. In answer to my silence he offered me his glass. "Want a sip? It will help you warm up."

Holding my hand in front of me, I shook my head. "No thank you. I don't drink."

"So tell me about you," Theeban said politely.

"Nothing to tell. I'm in my final year of high school."

"Really?" He sounded surprised. "You seem much older."

"Excuse me?" I asked, slightly offended.

"I don't mean you look older, like aged or anything. I mean by the way you act. You're kind of quiet and serious for a pretty high school girl." He moved in closer to me.

"Umm . . . okay . . . thank you, I think."

I heard a cell phone sound for an incoming text. It was Theeban's phone. I watched as he paused to read the text before slipping his phone back into his jacket pocket. A few seconds later, the phone buzzed again. This time it was a call. Theeban ignored it and turned his attention back to me.

"So what are your future plans?" he asked me.

The phone started ringing again. With a frustrated sigh, Theeban took out his phone and pressed cancel call.

"Sorry abou —"

The phone rang again. I could see a flash of annoyance cross his face.

"You know you can get that. I don't mind," I said politely.

"No, it's nobody."

"If a guy says it's nobody, then the person calling is a somebody. Most likely a girl." My voice was flat.

He looked at me in surprise. He wasn't expecting judgement from "a pretty high school girl."

I felt anger start to rise within me. But I quickly took a few deep breaths, calming the storm within. "Does your mom know?"

He shook his head. "Nah . . . well maybe. But she wouldn't approve."

"Why wouldn't she approve?" I asked.

"I dunno. She's not the type of girl my mom wants for me."

"Is she the type of girl you want for yourself?"

"I dunno," he repeated. "Even if she is, in the end it's who my parents approve of."

"Does she know that?" I asked, pointing at the phone. When he shook his head, I tried to hide what I was feeling from showing on my face. The poor girl. She probably thought she and Theeban were in love. "How long have you guys been dating?"

"A few years." When he saw my raised eyebrows he quickly added, "It's not really serious."

"You've been dating for a few years but it's not serious?" I was incredulous.

Seeing the shock on my face, he just smiled sheepishly.

I felt disgust overcome my anger. This time, I didn't bother hiding any of it. "Maybe you should be straight with her instead of leading her on. Or don't you think she deserves the truth?"

Without letting him answer, I stormed back to where my parents were sitting.

My anger flared up as I thought about Todd. He had confessed to liking me that evening in the shed. Then all of a sudden he was keeping his distance. In a way, I was grateful to meet Theeban and talk to him. There was no way I was going to be like that poor girl Theeban was playing with. I was going to get answers on where I stood with Todd whether he liked it or not.

16 A Little Patience

BY MONDAY MORNING, the anger and determination I had felt after the wedding had gone. I wondered whether I should stay home sick, even though I wasn't. Though, I might as well be since the anxiety at the thought of facing Todd was making me nauseous. I was starting the day with Creative Writing, and I didn't know how I was supposed to sit in the same room as Todd and pretend everything was great.

I realized I would have to face him at some point unless I wanted to change schools. But then I would have to come up with a reason to give my parents for wanting to do that. And I doubt avoiding a boy would count as good reason to them.

So, I was going to school. I made my way there, my heart thudding with nervousness. I was hyper vigilant, scanning for any sign that Todd was nearby. I entered the school and walked to my locker with slumped shoulders, trying to avoid being noticed. The gnawing in my stomach grew as I reached my locker and quickly got my things for class.

I almost jumped as hands touched my hips. I turned around quickly to see Todd. He was looking at me with a puzzled expression.

"Are you okay?" he asked.

I backed away from him, escaping his hands. "Ye . . . yeah. Sorry, you scared me," I responded. I pushed down the excitement I felt at his touch. Masking every feeling from my expression, I looked at him coolly. "What's up, Todd?"

His eyebrows furrowed in confusion. "What's wrong, Nisha?"

Not trusting myself to speak, I shook my head and continued to stare at him.

He rested his hand on the locker and leaned in closer to me. I pressed my back against the locker, trying to create as much distance between us as I could.

"Nisha . . ." he said in a deep voice.

"Yes," I squeaked. My heart leapt into my throat. I couldn't keep my body from responding as he brought his body closer to mine. I cleared my throat and pushed him gently away from me.

"Do you regret what happened last week at the shed?" he asked softly.

"Do you?" I asked him back.

"I asked you first."

"No. But considering that you haven't texted me or even talked to me made me wonder if you were having second thoughts."

"I didn't text you because I didn't want to rush you."

What did he mean by that?

He must have read the puzzlement on my face. "Nisha, we hadn't even gone on our first date. I thought it might be good to take it slow." He paused as he looked into my eyes. "But it doesn't mean I didn't want to."

I couldn't let him see how happy hearing that made me, so I maintained my blank stare.

Todd sighed. "I had wanted our first kiss to be special. I felt bad for making a move on you so soon without even taking you out. The next day I couldn't talk to you because I had to finish a group project. I hoped I would talk to you in class but you went and sat all the way across the room. And Friday . . . well I had a group assignment due last period. I had to spend any free time I had trying to finish it. I knew if I started talking to you, I'd never get my work done."

"So why didn't you just text me?" I asked.

"I don't like the idea of asking a girl out through text. I was determined to talk to you today."

I suddenly felt foolish for the way I felt over the weekend.

"Were you worried?" he asked.

"Nah," I lied. "I was just wondering that's all. I would hate for you to regret what happened and then have it be awkward between us."

He chuckled and grabbed my elbow. He ushered me forward. "Come on. Let's get to class."

Suddenly I felt light enough to run to class before the second bell rang.

The two weeks before our first date, Todd and I spent every possible minute we could together. Lunches were spent in secluded places, sometimes behind the staircase, hidden away from the students and teachers going up and down. Sometimes we met in the art classroom that was usually empty, except for one or two art students occasionally working on assignments. After school, if Todd didn't have to work, we would spend time in the library studying for midterms together.

Much to my disappointment, Todd refrained from kissing me again. He was stubborn about doing it properly. To him, that meant taking me out first. As much as I was frustrated by his chivalry, I also appreciated what he was doing.

Our first date finally arrived. I entered my house right after school and rushed up to my room. I had a quick shower and then stood in front of my closet wondering what to wear. I had told Todd I would meet him near the school at 6 p.m. I could only imagine what a disaster him picking me up at home would be. So I was taking my clothes with me and would change in the car.

I realized I had no idea what to wear on a date. After much thought, I settled on black tights, a grey and black striped thigh-length sweater, and knee-high boots. Folding the sweater into my tote bag with some makeup, I threw on a loose grey shirt underneath my jacket. I grabbed a few books and made my way downstairs. I heard my mother in the kitchen and called back over my shoulder, "I'm taking the car. I have a group assignment due, and we're meeting at one person's house to work on it." I felt a twinge of guilt for lying to her. But telling the truth would make me late for the date, or even unable to leave the house for it.

"Okay, keep your phone with you," was all my mom said without turning around.

Even though she wasn't looking at me, I nodded in response. I left the house and drove to the school. I parked the car in a darkened corner of the lot where I could change. I switched my shirt for the clingy sweater and tried to put makeup on using the dim light of the car. Grateful for good skin, I applied blush, eyeliner, and pink lipstick topped with lip gloss. I brushed my hair and put a dab of hair oil on my hands, rubbing it into my hair to make it smoother.

All done, I checked the clock in the car to see it was 5:40 p.m. I sat there, my hands fidgeting. I kept smoothing my hair and checking the car mirror to make sure everything looked good.

My phone buzzed and I rummaged through my bag to fish it out. It was a text from Todd: "Where are you?" I replied that I was at the back of the school.

Only a minute later, I heard a car drive into the parking lot and park a few feet away.

I got out of my car at the same time Todd left his. It was like we were magnets drawn together. We embraced each other in a tight hug and I felt a spark of anticipation for the evening ahead. We broke apart but our hands stayed entwined.

"You ready?" he asked.

"Where are we going?"

"Well there is a vegan restaurant that I always wanted to try. After that we could go to this art place next to it that allows you to paint ceramic items. Or —"

"That sounds cool. Where is it? Downtown?" I asked.

"No, it's in Markham."

"Oh . . . then no," I said slowly.

"You have something against Markham?"

"No . . . not really. It's just that I was hoping we could go somewhere . . . farther."

"Okayyy . . . can I ask why?" His brow furrowed in confusion.

"I don't want anyone I know to see me . . . us."
I made a gesture that connected the two of us. "The
last thing I need is for my parents to find out. Things
aren't that great with them right now."

"Aren't you allowed to date?"

"I dunno really. It never came up. They won't be
thrilled at the idea, but I think they care more about
other people finding out and the gossip."

He pondered for a bit, and then nodded. "Okay,
how about downtown?"

"Yeah, that's okay."

"There is a spoken word poetry show starting
at —" He paused to check the time on his phone,
"— six-thirty. We can go there and then figure out
what we want to do afterwards."

"Great! Let's go," I said. I was happy that he
understood. We got in his car and drove away, his
hand intertwined with mine.

17 First Date

"SO HOW ARE WE GOING TO WORK?" Todd asked me. We were walking hand in hand, strolling through the downtown streets after the show.

The show itself had been an amazing experience. We watched as people of all backgrounds came together in one space to share their struggles through poetry. It made me realize that oppression had many forms, but the feelings it caused were the same. I had left feeling stronger, knowing that I could also use my life to become my own person.

We were heading towards Dundas Square. A part of my mind registered mild surprise at the swarms of people around me at nine at night.

I was a bit surprised by Todd's question, unsure of what he meant. Seeing my confused expression he went on, "I mean if we are going to date and I can't be seen with you in public. How long do we have to be a secret?"

"It's not that we can't be seen in public. It's just that we have to be careful about how we act around each other."

"So . . . no public displays of affection?"

I nodded. I hoped the look on my face told him how much I regretted that.

"Damn." He pondered for a bit before he spoke again. "But why, though? There are a lot of other girls from your culture in school. And I know that they are not shy about getting affectionate in public."

I shrugged. "Dating is not the issue. It's the fact that you're not Tamil. Dating outside of the culture seems to get a few people's panties in a knot. Especially since I'm a girl. It's even worse because of the cultural stigma the girl has to bear. Boys can pretty much date whomever they please, even have sex. But girls are to carry the honour of the family."

"Seriously?" His eyes were wide in disbelief. "So if you're caught dating a white guy then . . ."

"I'm pretty much branded a whore by people outside my immediate family. Even if we're not sleeping together."

He let out a low whistle. "That's no pressure," he said jokingly. I let out a laugh.

"Don't get me wrong, there are Tamil women who date outside of their culture. It's nothing new. But it's especially bad with my parents. It's another drama because they're so strict with me. I'm a teenager and they might think I'm rebelling, which would be like the world ending to them. Maybe when I'm older, they'll leave me alone. But definitely not now."

"Since we're not in Scarborough anymore, I doubt we'll run into anyone your parents know. So

I guess I can do this." Todd stopped and pulled me closer to him, his arms wrapping around my waist as our eyes locked. He smiled at me and I smiled back, knowing exactly what he was going to do. My hands laced around his neck and I gently caressed the back of his head with my fingers. He brought his face down until his lips met mine. His lips were soft. The warmth of them sent what felt like an electric current down my spine. I pressed my body closer to his and he held me tighter as our kiss deepened.

And just like that the kiss was over. What happened? Why did he stop? Suddenly I became aware of our surroundings. Still holding me, Todd leaned his forehead to mine. His eyes closed as I stared at the gold zipper of his jacket.

"Are you okay?" I whispered.

"Yeah . . . I just . . ." he swallowed, his eyes still closed, "I just need a second."

"What's wrong?" I was worried. I tried to pull away but he clutched me tighter.

"Unless you want everyone in Yonge Dundas

Square to see what kind of effect you have on me, I think it's best for you to stay put. At least until I can calm down some parts of me."

"Wha . . . ?" As realization dawned on me, I stared at him, my mouth wide open. "Oh my god. I'm so sorry. But I didn't feeling anything —"

"What did you think you would feel?" he asked.

I clamped my hand over my mouth, completely mortified. "No! That's not what I meant. I mean, it's not like I know what it feels like, but it's just . . . I don't know." My incoherent babbling was not helping, so I decided to just stop. "I-I'm just going to shut up now," I said finally, looking down, feeling dejected.

I heard him chuckle. When I looked up, I saw his eyes were filled with amusement. He gave me a quick peck on the cheek, then grabbed my hand and pulled me to walk beside him. "Come on. Let's go. We need to get you home before your parents start to freak."

The drive back to the school parking lot seemed incredibly short. I knew I had to get home, but I wanted to spend more time with Todd. More time we didn't have to worry about people reporting on us back to my parents. Putting the car in park, Todd turned to look at me. "So, when am I going to see you again?"

"On Monday at school. Unless you want me to dish out more insults about your manhood sooner than that," I responded cheekily.

He grinned. His fingers smoothed the hair from my face. "You can insult me anytime."

I leaned forward to give him a quick kiss on the lips. As I went to pull away he brought me closer to him and kissed me again, this time longer and deeper. I groaned as his hands buried themselves in my hair. I felt my heart race and my hormones rage out of control. I knew if I stayed any longer things might get out of hand. So I quickly broke away. I put my hand on his chest to gently push him away.

"I have to go." My voice was barely audible as I tried to get my body under control.

He nodded reluctantly. "So I'll see you Monday first thing. Can you meet me a bit earlier than classes start?"

"Sure why?"

"Just because . . ." he trailed off.

With one final kiss, I got out of his car and made my way home.

18 The Storm Comes

I STARED AT THE CONFIRMATION PAPER in my hand. I headed downstairs to break the news to my parents. My relationship with them wasn't back to what it was before. I didn't think it would ever be the same again. There were times I would catch my dad staring into space with a look of sadness in his eyes that was quickly masked if he saw me looking. My mother, normally a vocal person, had gone quiet. The only sounds I heard from her were the quiet conversations she had with

Dad, which I could never hear clearly. It was a strange space for us to be in — I didn't like it. I wasn't sure if they were still mad at me or waiting for me to make the first move. So I decided it was up to me to test out the waters.

My dad was on his laptop in the living room and my mom was reading the newspaper while sipping on tea. As I walked in, they both raised their heads to look at me.

"I sent in my applications," I announced. My voice was devoid of any emotion.

"Which universities did you apply to?" my dad asked.

"McGill, University of Toronto, McMaster, Waterloo, and Queens," I answered.

"Good choices," my dad said.

"What programs?" my mom asked.

"No specific program yet. I want to take a few subjects and see what I feel like doing."

"No science courses?" my dad asked. "How will you get into medical school without studying science?"

I let out a sigh and went to sit on the couch. "I didn't say I wouldn't be taking science courses. But I don't want to focus on getting into medical school if that's not what I end up wanting to do. Who knows, maybe I'll do science but I'm not sure."

"Not wanting to go to medical school? Would you rather be an engineer? Or maybe a lawyer?" It was more words than my mom had said to me in two weeks.

"Maybe. Or maybe I want to be a teacher. Or a writer. Until I actually go to university and study, it's too early for me to tell," I answered.

"A writer? Who is putting these ideas in your head?" my dad asked. "We hardly see you anymore, and you never tell us about what happens at school." He frowned. "You're not seeing a boy, are you?"

I didn't say anything. I looked down, leaving their question unanswered.

"You are!" said my mom. "We want to meet him. To make sure he is from a good family." Then she looked panicked. "Unless he is not Tamil . . ."

My eyes widened in surprise. How had they guessed so easily? My mouth felt dry and my throat refused to let out any sound. I continued to sit there in silence, watching my parents freak out. Dread settled in the pit of my stomach.

"Nisha, tell us you are not dating a boy outside our culture," demanded my dad. "If you cause us shame . . ."

All my mother could do was wail at the very thought. "Is that why you've been out more than usual? We allow you this freedom and this is what you do to us," she cried out.

"Whoever this boy is, you will stop seeing him!" my dad commanded. "We didn't raise you to be a . . . a *vesai*!" he shouted.

I winced and my mother whimpered as my father compared me to a whore. But soon my hurt turned into a flicker of anger. Within a few seconds that anger turned into a raging flame.

"Enough!" I yelled. My breathing was hard and fast as heat filled every part of me. I clenched my jaw and stared at my parents, my eyes sparking with fury. I wanted to scream and yell at them. But the pain of my nails digging into my fists kept me from doing something I would be sorry about later. My eyes darted back and forth between my parents, taking in their shock. I was surprised to see something else in my father's face. Could it be sadness? Or shame.

My father looked away from me. Yes, it was shame at comparing his daughter to a whore. His shoulders were slumped and I knew that he had regretted his words as soon as they had left his lips.

I thought about how everything they had done for the last sixteen years had been for me. I felt my heart ache as I looked at them, the anger melting away. "*Amma*, *Appa* — I don't want you to think I'm disrespecting you. I just need you two to realize that I need to make my own decisions. I know you both think I'm a kid. But I'm never going to grow up if you always treat me like I don't know what I'm doing."

"We're not doing that, *chellam*. We —"

"Yes you are!" I cried out. I felt a bit of warmth and hope at hearing my dad address me with an endearment. "I need you both to trust that you've raised me well. Well enough to allow me to make my own life choices, whether you agree with them or not."

It was now or never. "I do have a friend. He's a boy, and he's not Tamil. We haven't done anything wrong. He respects me, and because of that he respects you and your wishes. He read my blog to understand more about our culture. He was the one who told me about the publisher looking for writers. I would hope you'd be happy that I had such a good friend."

My parents were quiet for a moment.

"We know," my mom spoke. "You're our only child and we want you to be successful. All of this . . ." She waved her hand around, taking in the whole house. "Every cent we have is all for you."

I walked over to my mom and knelt beside her seat. I covered her hand with mine. "*Amma*, I know that. And I appreciate all that you have done for me. But *Amma*, do you want me to be successful or happy?"

"Both," she said.

I nodded my head. "Wouldn't me being happy mean I'm successful?"

"Yes . . ." she responded slowly.

"Then let me find what makes me happy." I looked at my dad. "Even though I'm your child, I'm also my own person. I'll come to you for advice if I need it. But please . . ." my voice was pleading, "let me be allowed to make my own decisions."

My father patted the seat next to him, gesturing for me to come sit beside him. I eagerly went. As I sat down I leaned into his embrace as he wrapped his arms around me in a tight hug.

Rubbing my arm, my dad spoke, "I don't like the idea of you taking a chance with your future. I'm your father. How am I supposed to let go? But you're right. You won't grow up into a woman if we make all your decisions for you." He gave me a loving kiss on my head.

I choked back the tears that threatened to flow. I was warmed by the knowledge that I had such supportive parents.

19 Christmas Gift

THE FIRST SIGNS OF A WHITE CHRISTMAS came in the second week of December. It was the end of exams and students whispered in contained excitement as they looked out at the snow falling lazily outside the window. I had told Todd that I wanted to hold off on going on any more dates so I could focus on studying for my exams. So most of our time together was spent nose to textbook in the library or in Todd's hideaway. It wasn't the romantic time

145

together I had hoped for, but it was better than nothing. And it was useful to have someone to ask for help, especially when it came to Accounting and Geometry.

The last day of school before Christmas break I made my way to the mall. Being Hindu, my parents thought of Christmas as only a Christian thing. When I was little and still believed in the Santa Claus that all the other kids told me about, I had decided to put up my own socks along the wall in hopes that Christmas morning they would be full of presents. When I got up that Christmas morning, my heart burst with excitement and joy to see the socks filled with little toys. But as I emptied the socks, my joy turned to disappointment. My parents had used my old toys to fill up the socks, not knowing they should be new ones. That moment was when I stopped believing in Santa. I didn't care to receive any gifts after that. I walked around the busy mall that was teeming with shoppers, their hands full of shopping bags, walking from store to store. I felt out of place and unsure of what I needed to do or get. I had thought about getting Todd a Christmas present. But second thoughts overcame me. We had been seeing each other for only three months. Passing each store, there was nothing I saw that seemed just right. But then I caught sight of the bookstore. It was his love of reading that had brought us together. A book would be perfect. My fingers trailed along the shelved books as I looked at the titles. As if it had been waiting to remind me, my hand landed on *A Thousand Splendid Suns*. *That's it*, I thought as I went to look for a store worker.

"Excuse me, do you have any copies of *The Kite Runner* by Khaled Hosseini?" I asked her.

"Yup, it's right over there," she said. I followed her to a stand with books selected as favourites. With the book in hand, I went to grab a Christmas card and wrapping paper before heading to the cashier to pay. *Todd will like this*, I thought. I smiled to myself as I walked out with the first gift I had ever bought someone for Christmas.

Todd and I sat cuddling together on the sofa in his sanctuary. It was the day before Christmas Eve. His family was so busy with the holidays, I was glad for the chance to meet. "I got something for you," I said, lifting my head to look up at his face. I leaned into the warmth of his arm around me, my head resting on his shoulder.

He looked down at me and said, "I got something for you too." Todd went to the bookshelf and took down a small gift-wrapped box. I reached down for my bag at the side of the sofa and took out his gift. I had wrapped it in sparkling green paper and attached a red bow.

"You first," I said as I handed him the gift.

With an excited smile on his face, he slowly opened the present. His eyes widened in surprise as he saw the book.

"I know you said you liked his other book. So I thought I would get this one for you," I explained.

"I love it, thank you," he said as he kissed me on the forehead. "Your turn," he said as he handed me my first real Christmas present.

I stared at the gold wrapping for a few moments. I had a sudden overwhelming urge to cry. I slowly brought the gift up to my ear and shook it, trying to guess what was inside.

"Open it, silly," Todd told me softly. I stared at him for a few seconds. A few months ago, I never would have guessed I would be sharing a perfect Christmas moment with a boy I cared about. I felt myself drowning in the warmth of his gaze as a rush of emotions filled me.

"Todd I lo —" I stopped myself before I could say the words. I looked away for a moment, giving myself a chance to regain control. Then I smiled at him and turned my attention back to the gift.

I let out an audible gasp as I saw the royal blue box with the name Swarovski under the wrapping. I swallowed the lump in my throat as my fingers slowly opened the box. Inside was a crystal-encrusted swan hanging from a silver chain. I stared at it for what seemed like forever, taking in the beauty of the gift. Then I felt a little guilty when I thought about what he must have spent to buy it.

"Todd you really —"

Todd placed a finger on my lips, stopping my words.

"I know I didn't have to. But I wanted to. And when I saw the swan it reminded me of you."

"How so?" I asked, confused.

"Swans are very symbolic. The swan embodies purity of spirit, beauty, and faith. Things that remind me of you . . ." He trailed off.

"You could have gotten me a copy of the book *The Swan Princess* for a lot less money."

Todd barked out a laugh. Then he wrapped his arms around me in a tight hug.

"I could have," he responded, "but this is sparklier."

I grinned as I returned his hug. Bringing my face close to his, I whispered, "Thank you, Todd."

"So . . . you like it?" he asked.

"I love it," I whispered back as I brought my lips to his for a deep kiss.

Todd pressed me against his body. His hands ran up and down my back and I let out a groan as they moved down my thighs. I pulled my leg over him so I was straddling him on the couch. His hands gently lifted my shirt as I pressed myself closer to his chest, shuddering in pleasure as his fingers gently traced their way around my back.

"Nisha . . ." Todd groaned. His lips moved from my lips to my neck.

Suddenly, an image of my parents flashed through my mind. It stopped me in my tracks. A sense of frustrated disappointment flooded in. I tried to push myself off of Todd.

"Todd . . . I can't . . . not yet." I spoke reluctantly. My body seemed to reject the sanity of my words. I wanted him so much.

"Wha . . . ?" was all he said. His eyes were half closed. The evidence of his desire was obvious from the bulge in his pants.

I shook my head slowly. "I can't, Todd. I'm just not ready."

With the cloud of desire slowly fading away, I saw Todd slowly sit up straight on the couch. His hand ran through his hair as he tried to gather his composure.

Chewing on my lips, I looked at him. I felt awful about the whole situation. "I'm so sorry, Todd. I shouldn't have kissed you like that." I stopped when I saw his puzzled expression.

"Why are you apologizing?" he asked.

I shrugged, looking down at my fingers that were clasped together where they couldn't get into trouble.

He placed his arm around my shoulder and dragged me closer to him. With a finger under my chin, he raised my face to look at him.

"Nisha, I'm attracted to you. Very attracted to you. But that doesn't mean we have to do anything you are not ready to. You don't need to apologize every time I get excited," he said wryly.

I felt heat slowly fill my face. I gave him a shy smile and giggled. Then I let out a deep breath of relief. "I don't want to rush into sex without being absolutely sure about where we are heading. I don't want to disappoint my parents . . ."

Todd nodded. "I can understand that, especially if I have to be a secret." Hugging me closer to him, he gave me a soft peck on the lips.

"Oh, about that —" But then I decided I'd tell him later that he wasn't as much of a secret anymore.

"Only when you're ready," he said softly. At that moment I felt the love in his words penetrate my heart.

Epilogue

Students crowded the hallway, filling the air with energetic chatter as they waited to be called to start the graduation ceremony. I looked for Todd as I finished putting on my graduation gown. Frustrated by the amount of people in the hallway, I tapped my high heels impatiently. I checked my phone, my other hand holding the strap of my bag. The bag was weighed down by a hardcover book, which seemed to weigh a ton. I moved the bag to hang off of my shoulder and contemplated calling him. *Where is he?* I thought, my fingers ready to dial his number. I jumped slightly in surprise as I felt a familiar pair of arms hug my waist from behind. I turned with a huge smile, the impatience disappearing like it had never been there.

My bag slipped off of my shoulder and fell with a thud, spilling its contents onto the floor. "Oof!" I let out, "look what you made me do." I pouted as I bent down to retrieve my stuff. Todd helped me, his hand lingering on the book for a moment.

"Is this the . . . ?" he asked slowly, looking at me in wonder.

I nodded my head. "Surprise!" I said excitedly.

He stood up and eagerly turned the pages until he reached a page that had my name printed on it. "Oh my god, babe," he shouted. "There's your story. In print!"

He scooped me up in his arms and twirled me around. I threw my head back in laughter. I didn't care about the curious smiles directed our way.

"My girlfriend is a published writer," he said loudly as he put me down.

"That's your copy by the way. I thought you might like one."

I felt happiness fill me. When I had shown the book to my parents, they had looked at it with confused awe. They seemed unable to fathom what their daughter had achieved. But they were proud that their daughter had done something different.

I had kept the publication of my story a secret from my parents as well as Todd, wanting it to be a surprise. I also wanted it to be something just for me for a while. It gave me confidence and made me feel more certain of myself. With Todd's support, it had helped me make another decision. I had chosen a university to attend and the courses I would take. I went with my idea of doing a general first year, some science courses, some literature and history courses. To my surprise, my parents didn't object. They had hugged me and told me that they trusted my decision. Who knows, maybe I would be both a doctor and a writer.

I drifted back into reality as the principal called us to our seats in the front of the stage. When Todd looked my way, I mouthed to him, "I love you."

"I love you too," he mouthed back and we walked into the auditorium, hand in hand.

Acknowledgements

It is very difficult to be able to write without the support of the people around you. The time and dedication it took for me to complete this was only possible through the support of my family and friends. My immense gratitude goes out to my friend Missy Stone for not only offering but taking the time to read and provide feedback on my manuscript. You are a true friend!

I also want to thank my mother who pushed me to get this done, keeping me accountable every day and being a pillar of support. You knew what this meant to me and you wouldn't let anyone or anything else distract me from my goal. You are my hero.

A big thank you to my editor, Kat, for giving me this opportunity and being so patient this past year. Your kindness and understanding have been noted and very much appreciated.